Jessica Wollman

delacorte press

Published by Delacorte Press
an imprint of Random House Children's Books
a division of Random House, Inc.
New York

Delacorte Press and colophon are registered
trademarks of Random House, Inc.

www.randomhouse.com/teens

Educators and librarians, for a variety of teaching tools, visit us at
www.randomhouse.com/teachers

Library of Congress Cataloging-in-Publication Data
Wollman, Jessica.
Switched / Jessica Wollman. — 1st ed.
p. cm.
Summary: Laura and Willa, born the same night seventeen years ago on opposite sides of
Darien, Connecticut, are both unhappy with their lives and when they discover they
look remarkably alike, they decide to try out one another's lives for four months.
ISBN-13: 978-0-385-73396-0 (hardcover) —
ISBN-13: 978-0-385-90410-0 (Gibraltar lib. bdg.)
[1. Social classes—Fiction. 2. Mothers and daughters—Fiction.
3. Household employees—Fiction. 4. Boarding schools—Fiction. 5. Schools—Fiction.
6. Connecticut—Fiction.] I. Title.
PZ7.W8355Swi 2007
[Fic]—dc22
2006026426

The text of this book is set in 12-point Goudy.

Printed in the United States of America

10 9 8 7 6 5 4 3 2 1

First Edition

For my parents

Many many thanks to Wendy Loggia,
Pamela Bobowicz, Kendra Marcus,
Martha Jackson, Elizabeth Wollman,
Caroline Wallace, Martha Atwater,
Samantha Lee, Tiffany Aguilar, Mark Twain
and, above all, Daniel Ehrenhaft.

Prologue

On a hot summer night in late July, a daughter was born to a poor family. The mother named her Laura and cradled the baby in tired arms. The father did not want the child and spent most of the evening in a local bar.

On that same night, in the very same town, another daughter was born to a rich couple.

They named the infant Willa and wrapped her in white cashmere. Nurses fussed and fawned over the baby, while her parents planned her future. It would be glorious.

The two girls grew up. Side by side on life's timeline, they learned to crawl, walk and talk within hours of each other. And every year they celebrated their births on the very same day and in the very same town.

But although they were separated by only a few miles, the difference in their stations kept them apart. And so it passed that neither girl knew that the other existed.

1

*Mr. Clean cleans your whole house
and everything in it.*
—Mr. Clean Slogan

"Guess what happened this morning?"

Laura shook her head as her mother steered their battered station wagon through the posh streets of Darien, Connecticut. "I have no idea."

"When I woke up there were two crows on my windowsill." Laura's mother's voice practically fizzed with excitement. "They were just sitting there, staring at me. You know what that means, don't you?"

"We need to buy a bird feeder?"

Laura watched as her mother stuck her arm out the window to signal for a left turn. She tried to think of a time when the blinkers had worked properly, but she couldn't remember that far back.

"No, no . . . it's a sign!" her mother insisted, pulling her hand back inside and rolling up the window. "It means tonight's the night. It makes sense, too. The jackpot's up to twenty-four million. Can you imagine? Twenty-four *million*! Remember,

3

sweetie, you've got to play to win. Now we just have to choose our numbers, then after work I'll stop. . . ."

Laura shifted in her seat. How did her mom manage to be so upbeat? She stole a glance at her mother's hands. After years of cleaning and scrubbing, they were every bit as coarse and chapped as her own. But while Laura felt self-conscious about her perpetually chipped nails and red fingers, her mother didn't even seem to notice.

Laura glanced back at the familiar pile of cleaning supplies loaded into the backseat. She knew every product—their ingredients, slogans and effects—by heart. They were practically an extra appendage at this point.

How am I going to survive a full year of scrubbing toilets for the rich and not-so-famous? she wondered.

Laura Melon had grown up cleaning houses. Raised by a single mother, she'd been working for her family business—Darien Full Service Home Maintenance—since preschool. She didn't really have a say in the matter. Laura and her mom were the company's only employees.

Most kids dragged brooms and mops around the house, pretending to help their mothers. But Laura actually *did* help. She'd accompanied her mother on every job, helping her polish and clean the homes of their wealthy clients. By the time she was four, Laura knew how to get vegetable oil stains out of a tablecloth (don't rub, just sprinkle the spot lightly with baby powder, then launder). And when she was five, she'd stopped addressing her Christmas cards to Santa and switched to Mr. Clean.

The older Laura got, the more she cleaned. She cleaned after school, on weekends, during the holidays and over summer vacations. And somewhere along the line, she'd made an important discovery. Monumental, in fact.

She hated cleaning.

She hated the way ammonia made her eyes water. Hated how the work was so mechanical and mindless; she could clean an entire house without ever really turning her brain on. Hated having to stick her hands into other people's lives—touching their dirty clothing and half-eaten food. And most of all she hated the fact that, once she stepped inside a mansion, she instantly became invisible to its residents.

Laura glanced out the window. The homes were getting larger now, the front lawns more expansive, the grass rich and velvety.

The farther we drive from our apartment, the nicer the neighborhoods get. Laura pictured the musty two-bedroom apartment she shared with her mother, on the outskirts of a town famous for its estates. Their place was boiling in the summer and freezing in the winter. And no matter how hard they cleaned, it always looked dusty.

Laura wanted out. She had to leave. Because if she was miserable cleaning now, at sixteen, she couldn't imagine what life would be like at twenty-seven. Or thirty-seven. She had a plan, too. It was brilliantly simple. So simple, in fact, that the entire plan could be summed up in just two syllables: *college*.

If she had a degree, she'd be able to get a better job— something that didn't involve a scrub brush and a bottle of Fantastik. She'd probably even be able to help her mom out.

Yes, education was the only answer. Otherwise, Laura's hands might as well become Brillo pads.

She had the grades, too. Having taken every single Advanced Placement course available, she'd sailed through high school with a perfect 4.0. True, she'd spent all her free time working with her mom, so she had no extracurricular activities, but hey, she had a good excuse. Laura smiled as she thought of an Ajax-free four years. And then reality set in, coating the pleasant images like a thick layer of dust.

Her smile fell away as doubt rolled in.

Had she made the right decision?

The station wagon turned onto a long driveway lined with trees and paved with cobblestones.

Laura's mind wandered back to last fall, when her plans had begun to unravel. She and her mother had sat down and examined Laura's college account. The situation had been bleak.

Though her mother had tried to squirrel money away, life kept getting in the way—there were the station wagon's frequent trips to Midas, slow summers for the business, and cleaning equipment that decided to break at the worst possible moments—and she'd been forced to dip into the savings quite a bit. As a result, the balance was underwhelming. There wasn't even enough for Laura to attend UConn full-time for four years.

Her mother had urged her to take out loans, but Laura had refused. The money would have to be repaid—with interest—and Laura knew that her mother would feel obligated to help. She'd always worked so hard to avoid debt. How could Laura force it on her now, after all these years?

Looking for better news in the form of a scholarship or grant, Laura had met with her high school's college counselor,

Mr. Atkins. Sweet, sympathetic and stretched so thin he was practically transparent, the frazzled teacher had assured Laura that she was definitely one of his strongest applicants. Unfortunately, if she were to step outside of her own high school, she'd see that there were actually a lot of students like her: students with great grades, great test scores and great recommendations. They were all desperate to go to college and were also looking for the least financially painful way to get there.

Basically, everyone was fighting for the same baby pool of money.

"There just isn't that much to go around," Mr. Atkins had explained as he sifted through the contents of his bagged lunch and fished out a sandwich. "You don't mind, do you? Budget cuts. I don't get a real lunch break anymore."

Laura had shaken her head.

So, between healthy bites of a turkey sandwich, Mr. Atkins had suggested that Laura strongly reconsider her position on the whole loan situation. That was how most of his students financed college—especially with the current administration cutting out so much of the educational support system.

"You're a strong candidate, so there's a good chance that you'll get *some* aid," he said. "But between funding and your savings, you need to prepare yourself for some sort of gap." He swallowed. "Because it's going to fall on your shoulders to close that gap. And believe me, it can be quite large."

Never in her life had Laura felt more trapped. She'd always been strong. But now her resolve seemed to slip. Her bank account was small and, by extension, the world less accessible.

So Laura put her plan—and her mind—on hold for the year. She would graduate early and spend what would have been her senior year working full-time with her mother to save enough money for UConn. She had more than enough credits to get her diploma, and as for UConn, well, it was cheap, good and close to her mother.

When she broke the news to Mr. Atkins he shook his head. He still thought she was making a mistake about the loans, but in the end it was her decision. And at least she was *going* to college. At a high school that had a fifty-two percent graduation rate, Laura's was a success story.

So here she was. Laura Melon, full-time housecleaner. The problem was, it was only June and already she felt as if she were drowning in buckets of Murphy Oil Soap. Her mother had suggested she take some night courses to help the year go faster. At the time, random classes had just sounded depressing—Laura wanted to be a full-time college student, not a part-time one.

It's too late now anyway, she thought glumly. *Registration's closed at New Canaan Community.*

"Oh, oh . . . this is just gorgeous," her mother crooned. Her voice shook a little on each word as the station wagon bounced along the stone drive. "These new clients, the Pogues, they have quite a place."

"It's just a drive . . . ," Laura began, then stopped as the car approached its final destination. She looked up at the enormous Tudor estate and inhaled sharply.

With the ease of a seasoned professional, she quickly calculated the number of windows per floor. Her eyes ran up and down the grand facade, soaking up the impressive number of columns, turrets and wings. And then she exhaled.

It's gonna take forever to clean this place, she thought as she unbuckled her seat belt.

But on the bright side, at least the Pogues would be able to spring for their own supplies.

2

The debutante is the final result not
only of carefully paired bloodlines
but of schooling and coaching and,
of course, selection.
— *The Debutante's Guide to Life*

I was definitely switched at birth, Willa Pogue thought as she leaned back against the sofa's dark leather cushions, trying desperately to find a comfortable position. She was, once again, at her family's Darien estate, sitting in her father's study waiting for her world to finish falling apart.

It was a painfully familiar scene. Every time she disappointed or disgraced her family in some way, Willa's *presence was requested* at Pogue Hall. Once firmly ensconced in her father's wood-paneled study, she was then subjected to the now infamous "What it means to be a Pogue" lecture. Although Willa had heard the speech so many times she'd lost count, she knew it was the most common interaction she had with her parents.

"What's wrong with me?" Willa asked the room. Her voice bounced off the walls, disappearing into the dark oak. She leaned her head against a velvet pillow, then straightened. Her family crest was embroidered across the front. Yanking the plush cushion onto her lap, Willa narrowed her eyes slightly as she considered the bold red and yellow shield. There was also a Latin phrase scrolled across the crest, but Willa could never remember what it meant. And after a year of studying Latin in school, she still couldn't translate a simple sentence.

Willa sighed and shoved the pillow under her legs. She and boarding school just didn't mix. Actually, she'd clashed with *every* school she'd ever attended. Over the years she'd been "excused" from dancing school, equestrian class, elocution lessons and Gymboree (the teacher had insisted she was making lewd gestures). She never *tried* to mess things up—she was just really good at it.

So today, after she'd been called to the headmaster's office and handed her final report card—three big fat Fs and two incompletes—it had suddenly occurred to Willa that maybe she was simply leading the wrong life. Maybe she couldn't "get" being a Pogue because she wasn't actually a real Pogue after all.

Logic certainly supported her argument. As her parents lived to point out, the Pogues were known to excel. At everything. They all graduated from Shipley Academy—the esteemed institution where Willa had been floundering for the last three years—and then went on to Yale. From there, the sky was the limit! Name the field—politics, finance, academia—there was most definitely a Pogue outshining the competition at this very moment.

What Willa was never sure her parents completely understood was that the Pogues didn't hold a patent on the hyper-achievement gene. Boarding school was packed with Einsteins, Monets and Spielbergs, kids whose chief complaint was that the drudgery of class and homework got in the way of their extraordinary lives.

Willa, it seemed, was the exception to the rule. She *knew* she was mediocre. She didn't even really mind. She just wished her parents—and everyone around her—would leave her alone about it. And she wished that the path her parents had chosen weren't so *hard*.

One thing was certain. She was definitely *not* Yale material. She'd realized as much after flunking a fifth-grade social studies exam (when asked to fill in a map of the country, she'd left the entire Midwest blank—the Dakotas never made the six o'clock news anyway).

"I can see your grade-point average isn't the only thing you let slide this semester."

Willa snapped her head back up and found herself gazing into the icy eyes of Sibby Pogue. She could feel the dissection begin as her mother took a careful inventory of her hairstyle, weight and wardrobe, her gaze lingering over Willa's ripped jeans and worn flip-flops. Willa felt her cheeks flush slightly. It was weird how she'd grown up under her mother's harsh scrutiny but could never get used to it.

"You know," her mother said, her mouth twisting into a thin frown, "when I was your age I was never larger than a size two. Never. All my ball gowns had to be specially ordered. Did I ever mention that?"

About a thousand times, Willa wanted to scream.

But instead, she simply said, "Yes."

Willa looked at her mother, sleek and polished in a mint green cotton suit. Her black hair was pulled into a neat French twist, and round diamond studs glittered in her ears. Her light makeup was, of course, perfect.

Willa ran her fingers through her thick blond hair. She wasn't *bad*-looking—she knew that. She was nice and tall, and when people complimented her it was always about her hair or the green of her eyes.

But I certainly don't look like a Pogue, she thought.

She glanced down at her legs and swallowed as color crept into her cheeks and fanned out over her face and neck.

I am not fat, she reminded herself. *Broad does not mean fat.*

It was true, too. Willa knew that her weight wasn't really all that significant. If someone were to describe her—anyone in the world besides Sibby Pogue—it would never be in terms of her size. She wore a six in the summer and an eight in the winter, and she'd noticed that lots of girls in her dorm were around the same size, give or take a few pounds. Sure, she was no feather, but she was no elephant, either. Her hips and shoulders were solid and blocky, but if it hadn't been for her mother's constant digs, Willa wouldn't even have thought twice about the way she was built. Most people were even larger than she was.

But, of course, Willa was not most people. She was a Pogue. And Pogue women were ultrathin and elegant, yet strong and athletic, the sort of hostesses who could create a tasteful floral arrangement while playing mixed doubles.

Even though her mother hadn't been born a Pogue, Sibby fit right in. Willa, however, held the dubious honor of being the first large, uncoordinated heir in a long line of graceful, rail-thin, ultrasporty Pogues.

And her mother never let her forget it.

The study door opened and Willa's father entered the room, his brown suede loafers pounding the floor as he walked. He wore seersucker pants and a cashmere sweater that was just a few shades lighter than his hair. Willa knew her father was considered handsome—people were always telling him he looked like George Clooney—but she could never fully appreciate his looks. Not so much because he was her father as because his face was locked in a permanent scowl whenever he was with her.

Willa looked up at him. He was definitely in "deal-with-Willa" mode. His features were twisted into a tight glower and his cheeks were beet red.

"Congratulations," he said. "This was your lowest grade-point average ever."

Willa was actually kind of impressed that her father kept track of her GPA. She was always surprised when either of her parents knew anything about her—good or bad.

Her father glared at her, his nostrils flaring slightly. Willa shifted uncomfortably on the sofa, wondering if it would be okay to look away.

"Well, you've done it," he continued. "You do know that, don't you? Even with the family influence, Shipley doesn't want you back, and I'm not sure it's wise to push anymore." He raked a hand through his hair, and Willa watched as the strands fell neatly back into place. "Frankly, you've exhausted just about everyone involved here, Willa."

"I—I'm sorry," she said. "I went to the tutors and everything. I don't know—"

"It's not me you should be apologizing to," her father

snapped, cutting her off. "This is your future. And then of course there's the family to think of. You're not just anyone . . ."

For just a second, Willa wondered if her father expected her to send out some sort of apology to her dead ancestors. What technology did he want her to use? E-mail? IM?

She bit her lip. Giggling now—even smiling—would be wrong. So wrong.

As her father waded further into his speech, Willa tucked her chin into her chest. From this angle, she had no choice but to study her own feet. Thoroughly.

They were filthy.

I should have changed my shoes, she decided. *And my jeans. What was I thinking? I could've showered, too. I really have to—*

"Well—what do you have to say for yourself?"

Willa looked up, blinking at her parents in surprise. They were both staring at her. Each face wore a different shade of disgust.

Willa shook her head. She did that a lot—space out at the worst possible moments, like during exams or in the middle of intramural field hockey. Or when her parents were lecturing her about "What it means to be a Pogue." Her short attention span usually worked against her. In fact, Willa had a hunch it was a major player in her consistently poor academic performance. But today it had kind of come in handy. She'd heard enough stupid speeches to last several lifetimes.

The only problem was, there was a question hanging in the air and Willa had to answer it. And she had no idea what it was she was answering.

So Willa Tierney Pogue closed her eyes and inhaled sharply.

"I'm really going to apply myself at my new school because I know that's what we Pogues do. We see a situation and we go for the gold."

Willa waited for her parents to burst out laughing. How else could they react to her response? It was absurd. It was ludicrous.

"Good," her father said, turning on his heel. "Because I've been on the phone all morning with Bryce McCrady. He's on the board at Fenwick. It took some doing, but you'll start there in the fall. You'll have to repeat junior year. With your record, they wouldn't let you start as a senior. I strongly suggest you use your time at Shipley as a learning experience and start taking academics a little more seriously, Willa."

And then he was gone. Exit dissatisfied parent number one.

Willa stared at his retreating back. Fenwick Academy? Her head was spinning. In a single day she'd left one school and enrolled in another. She wondered how much of a donation her father had promised Bryce McCrady.

Actually, she didn't want to know.

Willa's mother straightened and cleared her throat. It was her show now.

"We're having the Havendales and the Todds over for lunch this afternoon," she said, her voice crisp and businesslike. Willa knew instantly that the "we" did not include her. "When I spoke to Bunny Todd this morning, she remembered that the Blakes have a son at Fenwick. We haven't seen them in years, but Caleb is about your age. I was thinking he could show you around, help you meet the right people . . ."

Willa listened to her mother silently, growing increasingly depressed by the moment. She could already see the entire year spread out before her, as wide and flat as an open stretch of highway. She didn't need a crystal ball or tarot cards. It didn't matter that she was switching schools. The year would be the same as any other. She'd show up, filled with all kinds of resolutions and promises: *I'm going to make lots of new friends this year! Get As, lose weight, and join the lacrosse team!*

And then school would start. The cliques would be impenetrable—especially for the new girl, who'd only been accepted because her father had bribed someone on the board. And—surprise, surprise—it's really hard to become a great student after years of being a total blow-off. This Caleb kid would be awful, too. She just knew it. Years of experience supported the claim.

The burden of being a Pogue was all-encompassing: it outlined not only a specific academic behavior but a social one, too. When she was younger, Willa's parents had rejected a number of her playdate requests for no specific reason. If she pushed, her reward was the "What it means to be a Pogue" lecture. After just a few attempts, Willa had learned to play alone or wait for her parents to extend an invitation to a more "acceptable" child.

Unfortunately, these children—always the daughters or sons of her parents' upper-crust friends—were nightmares. Willa still had the bite marks to prove it.

When she'd left for boarding school, her parents' influence hadn't waned. Over the course of her stay, they'd attempted numerous connections. Shipley was huge. There seemed no end to her parents' stock of "Pogue-approved" peers. They'd show up at random moments, grumbling and unhappy. And their introductions almost always began the same way: "My mom made me stop by. . . ."

Willa could never keep any of them straight. Because whether they were named Tristan or Coco or Greer or Caleb, they were all wieners. Total wieners. They were, in fact, the same little wieners they'd been when they were seven. Maybe they didn't bite anymore—though she couldn't be sure, since they never hung out all that long—but now their words took up where their incisors left off. The guys were always disappointed that she didn't fit the prep school mold—Willa had overheard one call her Wacko Pogue—and the girls were just plain snooty.

"So it's settled, then," Willa's mother confirmed in her usual clipped tone. "I'll ask Emory to find the Blakes' number. I think they summer in Nantucket, but I'm sure we have that address somewhere."

"I guess so," Willa said softly. She wasn't sure what else there was to say.

"I'm going to change for lunch," her mother said, turning to leave. "I'd ask you to join us, but I know you've got a lot on your mind. Emory has hired some additional help this summer—a cleaning crew—so I'll have him send someone up to unpack your trunk."

Willa watched her mother walk away.

It was all over. She was alone again.

She reached under her legs and pulled out the pillow. The

family crest stared up at her, those strange Latin words preten-
tious and taunting.

Clutching the cushion to her chest, Willa walked over to
the window and yanked it open a few inches. Using both hands,
she shoved the pillow through the crack and watched as it fell
softly to the ground.

She really hoped there was no language requirement at
Fenwick.

3

We work hard so you don't have to!
—Scrubbing Bubbles Slogan

Laura Melon was lost inside the Pogue Estate.

Her mother had dropped her off at the servants' entrance. "Go find Emory," she'd instructed before she drove off. "He's the Pogues' butler. I'll meet you just inside the kitchen."

It had all sounded so simple out on the driveway, but once inside the mansion Laura was greeted with total chaos. She'd arrived in the middle of preparations for a special luncheon and the pantry was in an uproar. A harried-looking cook was barking orders at an even more harried assistant, while a gourmet food delivery was being wheeled in.

Not wanting to get in anyone's way, Laura had walked away from the noise, toward the front of the house.

The place was mammoth and overwhelming. With every step, Laura felt smaller and smaller: a cat, a mouse, a fly. And worst of all, she wasn't sure *where* she was supposed to find Emory. Her mother hadn't been very specific.

So now she was stuck somewhere, swallowed by the estate, with no clue as to how to get back to the kitchen. And there was no one available to ask for directions.

Laura looked around, worry lines creasing her forehead. She was standing in front of a winding staircase (*always use Lemon Pledge on wooden banisters*) but she had no idea how she'd gotten there.

I should've stayed put, she thought. *I definitely don't need to climb stairs, because I didn't—*

"Look at you!"

Two bony hands sliced into Laura's shoulders and spun her around so forcefully that her thick blond ponytail circled her face, a long yellow whip. Laura steadied herself and stared up at the ultrathin woman. Her dyed platinum hair was almost white and she was wrapped in bright pink from head to toe. She looked like a walking pack of Carefree sugarless gum.

"Look at you!" pink lady repeated.

Laura could feel the color begin to creep into her cheeks. Speaking with strangers always made her nervous—especially fluorescent ones who accosted her in hallways.

"It's such an improvement!" pink lady gushed. Her pink-polished nails dug into Laura's collarbone. "I always *told* your mother that she should simply *insist*! No fights—just off you go! Hello, Frédéric Fekkai!"

Laura's mouth dropped open in surprise. The shock eclipsed the extreme pain radiating up and down her neck. *What?*

Pink lady tilted her head at Laura's ponytail. "But obviously you like it better this way, don't you? Now I can see your eyes!" She leaned forward with a conspiratorial wink. "I'm sure you break out less, too. Am I right? *Hmmm?*"

Laura tried to think of some way to respond, but it was simply impossible. What was going on here? And how was she ever going to get this woman to retract her claws?

"Excuse me, Mrs. Havendale, but the guests are in the sitting room."

A uniformed man stood in the hallway now and Laura's mother was with him. Laura's cheeks smoldered. She was seconds away from fainting.

Pink lady released Laura's shoulders and turned to the man. "Emory, I was just having a little talk with Willa—"

"Pardon my interruption, Mrs. Havendale," said the man. He cast a withering glance in Laura's direction. "But this is not Willa Pogue. This girl is a new member of our support staff—from a cleaning service."

Laura looked down at her feet. Was she supposed to apologize to the woman now? It seemed kind of stupid, but she wondered if Mrs. Havendale would blame her for the mix-up. Laura bit her lip. She'd feel terrible if she got her mother fired on their first day. And who was Willa Pogue?

But Mrs. Havendale looked too shocked to be angry. She just stood there, shaking her head. "It's so odd," she said. "I mean, I haven't seen her in a . . . but the resemblance—it's just so . . . ."

Emory stepped forward, placed a hand on Mrs. Havendale's elbow and nudged her gently. She walked off in a daze.

"Who's Willa?" Laura asked. Emory was staring, his eyebrows raised and his arms folded severely across his chest.

"Pogue Hall is *not* some sort of after-school hangout," he said, his voice biting. "When you arrive, you are to use the side entrance, then wait for me in the kitchen so that I can give you your assignment. Is that clear?"

"I tried—" Laura began. Then she stopped. She knew the rules. She'd been doing this forever. And at each house it was the same story. Emory didn't want to hear what she had to say. He didn't care that she'd actually looked for him. He didn't really think she had a brain.

Laura's gaze dropped to her feet again.

"I'm so sorry," she muttered. She'd only been at work for an hour and had already been totally humiliated. Twice.

Emory nodded curtly and the moment—in his mind—was forgotten. "After the tour we'll stop on the third floor so you can pick up your uniforms. You really shouldn't be wearing your street clothes inside."

Laura felt her stomach drop as she tried to catch her mother's eyes. "*Uniforms?*" she mouthed. "*Are you kidding?*" What was this, Victorian England? None of their other clients made them wear uniforms.

Her mother shrugged and tried to smile. *Maybe they won't be so bad,* her look suggested.

Emory started walking, motioning for Laura and her mother to follow. As they made their way down the opulent marble hallway (*any citrus-based cleaner works well on marble. In a pinch, squeeze a lemon into a bucket of Pine-Sol*), Laura noted how everything in the house—the rooms, the staircases and the corridor—was built on a much larger scale than any of the mansions she'd ever cleaned. The other homes were large; Pogue Hall was supersized.

It's like the Jolly Green Giant was their architect, she thought, stifling a giggle. She stared at the Pogues' music room. It was easily three times the size of her entire apartment.

Then there were the newspaper clippings. They were everywhere, framed and hanging from the walls. Every article featured someone named Sibby Welles. And they were all about thirty years old.

"It's impressive, I know," Emory said, pausing suddenly in front of one of the framed pieces.

Laura realized that she'd been staring. Her cheeks flared.

"Mrs. Pogue—her maiden name was Welles—was the toast of the Newport deb circuit," Emory declared as proudly as if he were talking about his own daughter.

Laura heaved a huge inward sigh. She'd seen this a million times before too—the help assuming that they were "part of the family." It explained Emory's haughty behavior and the way he was so protective of the house. He was suffering from serious delusions. This Sibby what's-her-face probably didn't even know his full name.

Emory continued with the tour. "The Pogues usually summer at the Newport estate, but they're back in Darien attending to an urgent family matter."

Laura thought she heard an undertone of discomfort edge into the butler's voice, but it vanished so quickly she couldn't be sure.

"They really don't use Pogue Hall as much as they used to, now that their daughter is older," he continued as they approached the stairs. "They'll be leaving for Newport again just as soon as possible. They spend the fall in New York and won't be returning to the house full-time until early spring. I travel with the family, as does the rest of the regular staff, so you see why it's important that we have people looking after the Hall in our absence. . . ."

Emory droned on in his polished, mildly bored monotone,

rattling off instructions about linens and deliveries—all of which Laura knew she should be trying to memorize—but she'd already tuned him out. There was a minicelebration going on in her head.

We have the whole place to ourselves until early spring, she thought. Sure, there'd probably be a few other hired guns and the occasional delivery person, but no rich, snooty family around to treat her like dirt. And empty houses were super-easy to clean. Of all the homes on her schedule, Laura had been dreading Pogue Hall the most. Now she was actually looking forward to her days in the massive, empty cave. It would be kind of fun. The summer, especially, would be a breeze. Business was slow, since most of Darien was on vacation—Pogue Hall was, in fact, their only regular job until Labor Day.

A pleasant rush of energy coursed through her, adding a fresh bounce to her step. Things were really looking up.

4

Be careful not to speak while eating a mouthful; it is indecorous in the extreme.
—*The Lady's Guide to Complete Etiquette and Perfect Gentility*
Emily Thornwell

The coast was clear.

Willa's eyes darted around the massive kitchen. Silver trays sat on a long wooden sideboard, ready to be carried off to the dining room as soon as her parents and their lunch guests were seated. She stared down at the delicate round finger sandwiches—paper-thin slices of cucumber wrapped around white bread.

"*Yuck,*" she said, wrinkling her nose. *Why would someone eat those on purpose?*

She turned quickly and shot over to the fridge. She didn't have time to hang out. She needed to grab her food and leave. Fast.

She yanked open the heavy refrigerator door and frowned at the oh-so-Pogue inventory: carrot sticks, fruit salad, low-fat cottage cheese and plain, fat-free yogurt.

She glanced back at the cucumber sandwiches as she let the door fall shut.

These can't be my only choices, she thought, desperately scanning the kitchen for a high-carb, high-sugar snack.

And that was when she remembered the butler's pantry.

She'd hidden a pint of Ben & Jerry's in that freezer over spring break. Someone might have eaten it in the interim, but at this point it was the only thing standing between her and flavorless yogurt. . . .

Willa sprinted into the tiny passage and whipped open the door. The cold air felt good against her face and she realized for the first time that she'd been sweating.

"*Yes!*" Her hand clamped down on the ice cream carton.

Walking back to the kitchen, Willa studied the icy container and frowned. The guilt was already setting in. While she could quiet her mother's critical voice when she was at school, in Pogue Hall it rang loud and clear whether Sibby was in the same room or not. The dull ache in Willa's stomach would seep to her bones by the time she reached the stairs.

I should really put this back, she thought. *I should eat something healthy—like a salad.*

Her heart began to pound. Whatever she decided, she had to do it quickly. If any of the regular staff walked in and found her holding a pint of Phish Food, she'd be in big trouble. Her mother had them on strict orders to deny her any and all junk food. Period.

And if Emory caught her—*ugh*. Just thinking about Emory made Willa's head pound. The guy loved telling on her. It was probably the only reason he got up in the morning.

Willa looked around. She was working herself into a semipanic.

And where *was* Emory anyway? It was weird that the kitchen was so empty when her parents were entertaining.

She glanced down at the ice cream again. The damp, smiling faces of Ben and Jerry peered up at her—so blithe, so carefree. *They* wanted her to enjoy their product, didn't they? She could have just a few, delicious spoonfuls in the privacy of her own room, right? What was so wrong with that? A girl her age could be doing so much worse. Why didn't her mother understand that?

Willa sighed. Ever since she was little her mother had bothered her about her weight. It had started subtly, with comments like "I wonder when Willa's going to get rid of her baby belly? She's the only one in kindergarten who still has one." By the time she was eight, all junk food and sugar were cut from her diet. Permanently.

Even then, Willa had known it was a ridiculous move. Impossible, even. The restriction was successful only in that it increased her appetite for *all* food—especially junk food. So she'd simply started smuggling the forbidden snacks up to her room. Since her parents barely spent any time with her—she couldn't remember the last time they'd even been to her wing of the house—the system had proven pretty much foolproof.

Willa's stomach growled. She hadn't eaten a thing all day.

I have the worst eating habits, she thought. She knew she tended to eat more—especially more of the high calorie stuff—when she was upset or stressed.

Like now, for instance.

Whatever. She was definitely going to eat the entire pint of ice cream upstairs in her room, alone. A depressing scenario, but at least it would taste good.

Just get upstairs, she thought. *You'll calm down; check in at MySpace. You'll feel better. You have the whole day to change around your site.*

At the thought, Willa felt her body relax. She'd discovered MySpace at boarding school. A few girls in her dorm had enjoyed discussing their friends—and thanking each other for adds—at an incredibly loud volume. They'd never encouraged Willa to sign up, but she'd visited the site anyway.

Six months later she had over fifty "friends" of all ages, from all over the world. Sure, Willa suspected that some of her "friends" were slightly less than honest in their profiles. For instance, three were leaving to tour with the All-American Rejects and five swore they were the illegitimate offspring of Axl Rose. Willa had done a little research and thought the latter claims might actually be possible—the guy had certainly lived—but it was hard to know for sure since none of her "friends'" declared ages were less than a hundred and five.

Whatever. Everyone was allowed to color reality a little, right? That was the beauty of MySpace. And even if they were lying, Willa's "friends" certainly beat her parents' lame fix-ups. Every day, she looked forward to reading about Roger's jerk of a football coach or Allie's new kitten.

Even Willa's profile was a little misleading. She went by a pseudonym—boardgirl—and didn't include a picture of herself. She kept her page purposefully simple: a few quotes ("Part of the secret of success in life is to eat what you like and let the food fight it out inside."—Mark Twain), a song from her favorite band, Lubé Special, and her list of friends.

What Willa loved most about MySpace was her lack of identity. She felt free online. Once she typed in her password, her towering family tree crumbled into a tiny pile of kindling. Boardgirl wasn't a Pogue. She didn't even know Willa. In the world of MySpace, Willa was as nameless and shapeless as an empty laundry bag.

And she loved it.

Reaching behind her back, she grabbed a spoon off the counter and turned to go, colliding with a woman—one of the maids. The ice cream slid through her hands and landed between them with a loud, damning thud. She bent over to pick it up.

"I'm *so* sorry!" the woman cried.

Willa was totally busted. Hiding her face behind a thick sheet of yellow hair, she stole a glance at the uniformed figure above her. The woman's light brown hair was streaked with gray; her round body looked solid. Willa didn't recognize her. Hadn't her mother mentioned that Emory had hired some additional staff?

Okay, Willa thought, her pulse calming. Maybe this really wasn't such a disaster. The new employees probably hadn't been briefed about her diet yet.

"No problem," she said, straightening. She tried to sound as smooth as possible. She held her ice cream as if she had nothing to hide. "I'm really the one who—"

"*Oh my!*"

The woman stared at her, a look of complete horror on her

face. Her mouth hung open and her eyes were rounder than the Oreos Willa hid at the back of her bedroom closet.

Color flooded Willa's cheeks.

Great, she thought. So Emory had already laid down the law. What did he do, pass out flyers?

"Fine," she snapped, rolling her eyes. "I'll put it back. I'm not having one of those gross vegetable sandwiches, though."

"No, no." The woman spoke slowly as if in a trance. "It's your face—you look . . ."

Willa shrugged. "Look, it's just ice cream. I think its *chocolate* that's supposed to give you zits." She smiled wryly. "Besides, we *Pogues* don't even get zits. Or didn't Emory tell you that?"

The woman cleared her throat. "It's just that you look like my—well, I suppose it's not important. . . . Now, you poor thing, your ice cream is melting. Let's get you a bowl for that, shall we?"

Willa blinked. This sudden generosity really caught her off guard. The staff wasn't usually very friendly. They seemed to follow her parents' lead and treat her as if she were on some sort of permanent probation.

"I'm Andrea Melon," the woman continued as she scooped Willa's ice cream into a large bowl. "But you can call me Andy. I just started working for your family today."

"It's, uh, nice to meet you," Willa said.

She was about to ask Andy why she'd been so spooked, when she heard footsteps in the hall. Willa's heart started to thump again. She'd better not push her luck. It might be Emory. She, Ben and Jerry had to get up to her room.

"Listen, I know you're busy—what with my mom's guests

31

and all," she said, reaching across the table to grab her ice cream. "So I'll just get out of your way, okay?"

The older woman placed her hand on Willa's arm for a split second. It felt warm and reassuring.

"You're not in my way at all, dear," she said. "But you do what you like. It's such a pretty day out. I'm sure you have lots of fun things planned."

There were voices attached to the footsteps now.

Willa had to go. Immediately.

She held up her free hand in a light wave. "See ya."

Andy turned and winked at her, the skin around her eyes wrinkling sweetly.

Willa slipped up the back stairs, narrowly avoiding Emory. As she climbed the steps, she thought of Andy's comment—*I'm sure you have lots of fun things planned.*

Sure I do, Willa thought as she opened the door to her bedroom. The air felt thick and stale. *What's more fun than spending a little quality time at MySpace with Ben and Jerry?*

5

So Clean You Can See Yourself
—*Formula 409 All-Purpose Cleaner*
1977 Ad Slogan

Laura stepped inside the blue bedroom and stared at the wide plank floors. They were hand-painted; the tiny blue and yellow flowers matched the blue-trimmed walls. The sun streamed over the rich whitewashed furniture and, in the back of the room, a sky-blue window seat was piled high with plush cushions. Emory had mentioned something about the Pogues' having a daughter. This must be her room.

As far as assignments went, she could do worse. Her mother had gotten stuck with the rest of the staff serving the Pogues' lunch guests, while she was here to unpack an obscenely large trunk. It was boring, but she was alone; she could work at her own pace.

She scratched her neck. If only her uniform didn't *itch* so much. She'd probably get a rash.

At least she'd been wrong about one thing: The uniforms hadn't smelled. They just felt as though they were made of straw.

Laura allowed herself to imagine, for just a few seconds,

what life would be like if this were *her* room. She pictured herself relaxing on the window seat, doing some light reading, or finishing a paper at the elegant six-drawer desk. If this were her room, she'd never have to think about money—not ever. And she could use any shower in the house without worrying about having to scrub it later on *(Scrubbing Bubbles is the best on soap scum. Don't let anyone tell you otherwise)*.

If this were her room, she'd be leaving for college in just a few weeks.

"Whoever lives here has a perfect life," Laura informed the empty room. Her voice caught a little in her throat.

Her eyes drifted over to the bed. It was covered with throw pillows, each with a different motivational slogan embroidered on it—YOU CAN NEVER BE TOO RICH OR TOO THIN!, LOOKING GOOD IS FEELING GOOD! and YOU ARE WHAT YOU EAT!

"This Pogue kid must be a real—" Laura said, and then froze. There was a picture on the bedside table in a thick silver frame.

It was a picture of her.

Well, it wasn't exactly her—but it was close. The complexion was the same: blond hair, green eyes and skin unusually dark for someone with such fair hair—people were always asking Laura if she used a spray-on tanner. The soft, round nose was identical too—even down to the light splash of freckles across the bridge. She wore her bright blond hair down, while Laura's was pulled into a ponytail. The similarity was amazing.

Laura thought back to her run-in with the pink lady—Mrs. Havendale. She'd just assumed that the woman was a little strange—her outfit certainly was—but now her reaction made sense. She'd mistaken Laura for the Pogues' daughter. She'd called her . . . what was it?

"Willa," Laura said to the picture, her memory suddenly returning full force.

She scanned the room, then frowned, disappointed. There weren't any other pictures hanging up. How tall was Willa Pogue? What shoe size did she wear?

Laura walked over to the bookshelf. It was stuffed with yearbooks, pennants and pins from Shipley Academy. She pulled a book off the shelf and started to flip through. She couldn't remember the last time she'd been this excited.

"Willa Pogue . . . Willa . . . where are you?" she muttered. She noticed that the girl's yearbook pages were just as empty and unsigned as her own.

So that's another thing we have in common, Laura thought. *Neither of us are exactly A-listers.*

"What are you doing?"

The voice that pierced Laura's thoughts matched her own down to the very last cadence, tone and intonation. It was as if there were a recording of her playing somewhere in the room. She was so startled that she dropped the yearbook and spun around.

Willa Pogue looked exactly like her, Laura noted with some satisfaction. It really was amazing. They were like socks from a matched pair. Looks were looks. She and Willa shared the exact same height and features. They had the same coloring, too.

Except for now, of course.

Willa was purple with fury.

And Laura was red with embarrassment.

"I—I'm so sorry," she stammered. She stared hard at Willa, waiting for her to realize that they were basically identical in every way. She figured that would help smooth things over.

"Emory sent me up here to unpack your trunk," she explained, but as she said the words she realized the excuse sounded painfully lame.

"Oh, and you thought the key would be in one of my yearbooks?" Willa said, her voice thick with sarcasm.

Laura shook her head and tried again. "Look, I'm sorry. I was just interested. I didn't mean to—"

"Oh, forget it, just shut up," Willa snapped, her eyes flashing. "Go ahead—you already started. Look at everything, okay? I don't even care anymore."

Then she stomped off.

Laura sighed as she bent over to collect the fallen yearbook.

"Well," she said, softly, "at least I learned more about Willa Pogue."

6

In speaking to a servant, either a lady or a gentleman will ever be patient, courteous, kind, not presuming on his or her power.
—*Manners and Social Usages*
Mrs. John M.E.W. Sherwood

As Willa stormed out of her bedroom and down the hall, several thoughts ran through her head:

(1) Now the maid knew she was a total loser.

(2) The new maid was a thinner, prettier version of herself.

(3) Her ice cream was all melted.

Although number three was upsetting, one and two were far more disturbing.

She dropped down on the top of the steps and gave the ice cream a small shove, not bothering to hide it. She was way too miserable to care if Emory caught her.

How much did that maid see? Willa thought, burying her head in her hands. Why hadn't she put those stupid yearbooks away? Or better yet, just tossed them out? They made her feel like such a loser—and she felt like one on a pretty regular basis anyway. Besides, she was barely in them. She wouldn't have even ordered them, but they were included in the price of school tuition. Every year they'd simply been shipped home automatically, so she'd stuck them on her shelf.

Why did I leave that stupid twig alone in my room? Willa thought, her eyes fierce. *It's my room! And why do I even care what she thinks?*

Willa raced back to her bedroom. The girl was standing over the open footlocker folding a shirt. When she saw Willa her mouth fell open but no sound came out.

"Get out!" Willa snapped. *"Now!"*

Had she ever yelled like this? It felt strange to hear her voice this fierce, this angry. Even she knew she sounded insane, but she couldn't seem to stop herself. Just looking at the girl, so neat and trim, made her feel like punching the wall.

The maid dropped the shirt and rubbed her hands together, as if they'd been burnt.

"I can't," she said, her cheeks turning pink. "I have work to do in here and if I leave I'll—"

"I don't care!" Willa shouted. "This isn't your room, you know. I live here!"

The girl's face suddenly lit with anger. "Look, do you think I *want* to be here?"

Willa instinctively took a step backward. "What?" She couldn't tell what had surprised her more—the girl's rage or the fact that her wide-set eyes matched her own so perfectly.

"You heard me. It's not like I *chose* to be here, you know," the girl said. She raised her arms in a grand, sweeping gesture. "Do you think this is *fun* for me? Well, here's some news: unpacking your disgusting trunk isn't a thrill. But I need to work so that I can pay for college. Not like you'd ever understand that."

Willa watched, stunned, as the girl picked up the dropped shirt, refolded it and placed it neatly on the bed. The movements were practiced and fluid.

Standing in the doorway, Willa was suddenly unsure of what to do or say. She was—for the second time—a guest in her own bedroom. After a few minutes, she silently turned and walked down the hall. When she reached the stairs, she sat back down on the top step, next to her now-liquefied bowl of Ben & Jerry's.

And then Willa curled her body into a tiny ball and burst into tears.

7

"You're soaking in it."
—*Madge the Manicurist,*
Palmolive Commercial, 1966–92

We're definitely getting fired.

Ever since Laura's showdown with Willa Pogue, the thought had become her mantra.

She'd totally blown it yesterday. What was she thinking, telling off a member of the family? Laura had never done anything like that on a job. Of course she was going to be dismissed. She was surprised it hadn't happened last night.

Laura looked at her mother, and a bubble instantly formed in her throat. She'd wanted to prepare her, but her mother had been in such a great mood when they'd gotten off work. She'd run off to bingo at the community center and then cooked a late dinner in celebration of their new job—and what she was certain were her winning Lotto tickets. She'd lost, of course, but even that hadn't dampened her spirits. And Laura had wanted her to go to bed happy.

But now, standing beside her mother in the Pogues' massive kitchen, Laura knew she'd made a mistake.

I should have apologized, she thought. *This is my fault. All my fault.*

Emory cleared his throat.

Laura held her breath.

"We're leaving for Newport tomorrow—Mr. and Mrs. Pogue and the regular staff. We're packing up the Pogues' travel car now. It'll take the rest of the afternoon." The butler looked around the spotless kitchen. "There's so much to be done. I'll give you your assignments for the summer and then I'm off. . . ."

Why wasn't he yelling at her? He was acting as if he had no idea that she'd had a huge, screaming fight with Willa Pogue. But that was impossible—wasn't it?

". . . her room needs to be cleaned, her closets combed through because they're in a state and her dressers relined."

Laura tuned back in to the conversation to find that Emory was now staring directly at her, rattling on about something—or someone.

"Her other trunks arrived from school late last night, so once you're finished with the first, you can get started on those," the butler continued.

Laura's body tensed as she began to understand the "what," and "whom," Emory was talking about.

"Listen, I'm not sure—"

"Everything needs to be repacked for school in the fall, of course," Emory pushed on, as if she hadn't spoken. "And you'll have to work around her since it has been decided"—at this, Emory slid his gaze just over Laura's head—"that Willa will not accompany her parents to Newport." He cleared his throat.

"But that's fine. Winter clothes are on the third floor. Cashmere is kept separately. . . ."

This is worse than getting fired, Laura thought, her head swimming. Willa Pogue totally hated her, and now she was stuck in the girl's room all summer? What kind of terrible karmic retribution was this? So, she'd snooped through the kid's yearbook because they were look-alikes. Some cleaning people stole things! She'd even met one woman who tried on her employer's clothing—right down to her underwear. Laura would never do anything like that.

And what sort of parents packed up an entire house for summer vacation but left their daughter behind?

"Sweetie, are you okay?"

Laura looked up. Her mother was leaning toward her, a concerned look on her face. Emory was gone.

"Would you mind changing jobs with me?" Laura blurted. "I don't think Emory will care as long as it gets done. I'll take all of the other bedrooms if you'll take the Willa job? Please?"

"Oh, come on, sweetie. I work faster," her mother said. "If I switch with you it'll be harder for us to get out on time."

Laura shrugged. "I don't mind staying late. Really."

"Well, the thing is, I'm going to the movies with a friend I met at bingo. Dr. Pool—you must have seen his van around town? He's picking me up after work."

Laura stared at her mother, frowning slightly.

A movie? With that pool repair guy? Was this a date? Laura scanned her memory, trying to remember if her mother had ever mentioned Dr. Pool before, but she came up empty.

Her mother grinned as if everything was normal. "So really,

let me take the heavier load, why don't you? Besides, Willa's your age. I can see you two really hitting it off."

"Listen, Mom. Um, I never told you about this thing that happened yesterday when I met Willa—"

"I know exactly what you're going to say."

Laura looked at her. "You do?"

"Uh-huh. I met Willa yesterday too. It's amazing how much you girls look alike. I just couldn't get over it." Her mother paused. "But I got the feeling she isn't very happy."

Laura shook her head in disbelief. Her mother actually felt bad for that *brat*?

"Right," she said, recovering. Her mouth tingled with sourness. "I'm sure she's miserable. I'll bet she cries herself to sleep every night in that huge, amazing room. Or maybe she hops from room to room? She could, you know—a different room every night of the year."

Placing a hand on her arm, her mother squeezed gently. They stood that way for just a few seconds. Laura could feel the warmth from the work-worn skin as it fanned over her, wrapping around her body like a knit blanket (*to launder: always use Caldrea Delicate Wash, gentle cycle, then line dry*).

"Time to go to work," her mother said.

Laura trudged up the stairs, lugging her cleaning caddy toward the blue bedroom.

What a nightmare. The summer hadn't even officially started and she could already mark it down as the worst of her entire life.

But why am I still here? Laura wondered again. *Why didn't Willa tell on me?*

Maybe the girl was planning on blackmailing her. Laura smirked as she pushed open Willa's bedroom door. That was too ridiculous, though. She sighed. Maybe her mom was right. Maybe she'd misjudged the girl. Maybe Willa Pogue was human after all.

Something snapped against her kneecap.

She looked down and realized that she was standing in the middle of a hair accessory minefield. They were everywhere: clips, bands, barrettes and brushes. There were hundreds of them.

The empty room reminded Laura of a movie scene: Character returns home to find that everything has been destroyed by mobsters or Secret Service agents in search of something important.

In less than twenty-four hours, Willa Pogue had taken a relatively neat bedroom and transformed it into a hard hat—and knee pad—area. Every single drawer had been pulled from the dresser and dumped onto the floor. Sheets and pillows were also on the floor, as was a very expensive-looking laptop. The television was blasting at a volume even the local nursing home would find offensive.

Laura clicked off the TV. *Did Willa do this to get back at me? It doesn't make sense. Why wouldn't she just get me fired and be done with it?*

Forget it, she told herself. *You don't know her. She might be a real sweetheart.*

Laura repeated the same line when she opened Willa's closet and was pelted with a month's supply of dirty socks.

And again—but with much less enthusiasm—when she

unlocked Willa's second trunk to discover that the heiress had packed her shampoo and conditioner without their caps.

Who does something like this? she wondered as she wiped her soapy hand against a rag.

And then there was a pounding in the hallway, just outside the door.

"Ladies and gentlemen, I think I have my answer," she muttered as Willa Pogue herself barged into the room.

"You! Why are you always here?"

Laura sighed and turned to face her very spoiled employer.

Let the good times roll, she thought.

8

The dress of the young debutante must be
simple and tasteful.
—*Youth's Educator for Home and Society*

```
lubespecial: u there?
boardgirl: yep. but am boredgirl from
now on, ok?
lubespecial: y?
boardgirl: shopping with my mom.
lubespecial:  thought  girls  liked
that?
boardgirl: NO. NOT THIS 1. HATE IT.
lubespecial: ez there. am w/u. been
wearing same jeans since i wuz 12.
boardgirl: TMI. sounds like i shld
p/u new pants 4 u. size?
lubespecial: wait. pants cum in sizes?
boardgirl: no clu, wanna talk 2 my mom?
```

"Willa, put your phone away. It's just so coarse, typing like that."

"Coarse" was Sibby Pogue's favorite word. It was the adjective she used to define people and behaviors she considered low class: anyone who did not play golf and tennis, short men, women who drank beer, wearing diamonds before noon, mothers who breast-fed their children any place other than a nursery, children who did not attend dancing school . . . The list was endless and frighteningly specific. Willa was certain that, over the years, her mother had labeled every single human being—and some animals—as coarse; Sibby Pogue being the one exception, of course.

Stuffing the phone into her pocket, Willa sent a telepathic apology to Lubé for cutting out so abruptly. She'd write later and explain.

Lubé was Willa's one MySpace friendship that had actually evolved past the confines of the site. They'd met when he'd invited her—and about eighty other random people—to be his "friend" in an attempt to spread the word about his band, Lubé Special. Out of boredom, she'd added him to her list and streamed one of his songs, "Tune Out." After only an hour, she'd learned every word, beat and chord by heart. She even caught herself air-guitaring a few bars of the solo.

The entire experience had caught Willa by surprise. She was not, by nature, a music person. Not by a long shot. She didn't frequent iTunes, didn't watch MTV. She rarely listened to the radio. But overnight, all that had changed. She'd become a regular Lubéhead (not an official band term. Later on, Willa did mention it to Lubé but he was horrified and strictly forbade its use).

Despite her miniobsession, Willa had been hesitant to contact Lubé. For the first time ever, she actually felt intimidated by someone on MySpace. Not only was Lubé enormously talented, but he just seemed different than her other "friends." Even his site was different, since it was on MySpace Music. He didn't post pictures of his pets or list his favorite TV shows. Lubé's profile was even sparser than Willa's: no picture, he went to public school in San Francisco, and he was the singer and lead guitarist in Lubé Special. He did list a few musical influences, but that was as personal as he got.

Willa knew right from the start that Lubé's interest in MySpace was strategic rather than social: He'd opened an account to promote his band. His three hundred and twenty "friends" weren't really friends at all; they were fans. He never changed their ranking or commented about them. Except for posting new songs and band news, Lubé's page never changed.

The truth was, Lubé didn't need MySpace, not like Willa. He wasn't lonely. And that fact intimidated her way more than his music ever could.

So rather than risk rejection, Willa had settled for memorizing Lubé's profile. Sure it was thin, but it was her only connection to the guy with the haunting voice. Besides, boiling him down to a few concrete facts, folding him up into a nice neat carryall, was oh-so-appealing. Appealing and safe.

But midway through her research, Willa's plan hit a snag. Lubé claimed to love a band called the "Sins," but when she searched for them, she kept winding up at the Vatican's Web site. It happened so many times that her frustration eventually eclipsed her anxiety. One night, late, Willa e-mailed Lubé. She figured he'd never respond, but by then she didn't care. She was pissed at the guy for sending her on such a wild-goose chase.

Lubé responded immediately. He apologized for the typo; the band was called the *Shins*, and he was ecstatic that Willa was open to listening to them ("My friends wouldn't let me play them *one* song," he'd complained). He also had no idea that the Vatican had its own Web site. How creepy is that? he'd written.

Willa and Lubé had been in contact ever since. They kept things light, never getting too personal. For instance, Lubé had no idea that Willa was switching schools and she had no idea if he had a girlfriend. But their conversations were frequent—almost daily—and Willa found herself looking forward to them.

She also found herself wondering what Lubé looked like. She liked to picture a younger version of Gael García Bernal, but she knew that was just wishful thinking. Once she searched online, but she came up with nothing. It was stupid, she realized afterward, since she doubted Lubé was even his real name.

It was just as well anyway. Public school and in a band. As far as Sibby Pogue was concerned, Lubé was sandpaper.

"Here we are."

Willa looked up and flinched. *A Perfect Paradise*. Her mother hadn't mentioned she was taking her here, but where else would they go? If you were Sibby Pogue, clothing was purchased here, in this store, behind this hot-pink lacquered door. The Gap and Old Navy did not exist.

Willa was trapped in Paradise. With her mother.

According to the store's owners, paradise was neon pink; the national tree, the palm. Willa stepped onto the thick green carpet and swiped at her eyes. It was just so bright in here.

A pretty blond saleswoman approached. Actually, her perfume approached first. "Mrs. Pogue! It's so nice to see you. And you've brought your daughter. Looking for something special today?"

When her mother spoke her voice contained not a drop of warmth. "Yes, thank you. My daughter needs some more-appropriate things than what she seems to be favoring at the moment. Pants—no jeans. Cashmere sweaters, if they're in yet. No black, please." She glanced at her watch. "I'd like to be done here in a half hour, if that's possible. My husband and I leave tomorrow for the entire summer and I have quite a few errands. . . ."

It suddenly occurred to Willa that the saleswoman had learned of her parents' plans at about the same time she had. Willa's mother had only broken the news to Willa earlier that morning, when they were leaving Pogue Hall.

She'd also made it perfectly clear that Willa wasn't invited.

"There are too many distractions in Newport," her mother had explained. "Your father and I feel that you need to focus on next year, concentrate on your summer reading; really prioritize. We'll be back and forth to check in, of course. Plus, we'll have staff around so you'll hardly be alone."

Willa had said nothing. She knew better than to argue with her mother. Besides, she hated the snooty country club scene at Newport—it was like a boarding school convention up there. If she went, the summer would be nightmarish.

But it was always nice to be asked.

"Excuse me? Miss?"

Willa looked up and realized that the saleswoman was staring at her, an expectant look on her face.

"I'm sorry," Willa said. "What was that?"

"What size do you wear? It's easier that way. I'll just bring
the clothes to you."

"She's a size thirty-eight." Her mother's eyes narrowed. "At
least."

Willa felt the color rush to her cheeks. She wanted to correct the statement, but she could never keep the European sizes
straight. Was a thirty-eight an eight? Or was it more like a six?
And why couldn't they just go to Abercrombie & Fitch?

"Um, sure. We've got some great things in for fall. Let me
just get some outfits together. . . ." As the saleswoman turned
away, her eyes met Willa's. In the silent exchange, Willa de-
tected an undertone of sympathy.

Is my mother any worse than the usual? Willa wanted to ask.
Do you see this all the time?

On the other hand, maybe it was best not to know.

Ten minutes later, Willa looked like an Easter egg. At least
from the waist up. From the waist down, it was *Martha Stewart
Living* all the way. She was on color overload and it was giving
her a headache.

Standing in the tiny, Pepto-Bismol-colored dressing room,
Willa studied her outfit: a bright pink and yellow cashmere
sweater paired with navy slacks.

It was no use; she might as well tell her mother now. She
could wear Pogue-friendly clothing dyed all the colors of the
rainbow, but what would it matter? It wouldn't whittle her

shoulders or narrow her hips. Her heavy blond hair wouldn't magically turn sleek and black. She'd still have the same thick, arched eyebrows; the same wide green eyes.

Everything in this store always looked strange on her. If anything, the clothes seemed to emphasize her un-Pogueishness.

Plus they *itched*. Willa glanced down at her outfit. From head to toe the ensemble was one hundred percent cashmere, but *wow* was it uncomfortable.

I will never ever wear this, she thought.

The door swung open—her mother never bothered to knock first—and Willa shifted her weight from leg to leg as her mother's eyes locked onto her.

"We'll take this one," her mother said. "We'll buy the sweaters in different color combinations too. Light colors."

Tell her. Tell her that you hate this place and all the lavender twinsets you've bought here. Tell her that you like black. Tell her that you want to shop someplace else. Vintage sounds cool. . . .

Willa's mother clicked her tongue impatiently. "Honestly, Willa, don't just stand there like a lump. I've got a million things to do today. Give me the clothing and let's get out of here."

There was steel in her mother's voice.

On the other hand, there was something to be said for not making waves. She could always go home and bury the clothes in the back of her closet and then take a nice, long nap. That might erase this whole pastel catastrophe.

She was shrinking into herself. This always happened.

Why are you such a wimp around your parents? You were strong the other day, fighting with that girl. Okay, maybe you crossed into psycho territory, but you definitely got your point across.

"Did you hear me? Hand me that clothing so I can pay. I'm meeting Tinsley at the club and I need to take you home first. Willa!"

Looking down at her feet, Willa felt her arm unfold, extending itself.

She wasn't strong. Not when it mattered.

Willa handed the rest of the clothes to her mother. Even though it was eighty degrees outside, Willa wore the cashmere sweater and pants home. She was too tired to change. Ordinarily such a move would have provoked her mother, who considered dressing out of season an extreme act of terrorism, but Sibby was in such a rush that she didn't seem to notice. When she dropped Willa off at Pogue Hall, she barely even stopped the car.

Willa ambled up the steps on tired legs. Wet clumps of wool clung to her body and hot pink packages banged against her legs.

She was melting. Definitely melting. Not changing had been a mistake. Willa yawned loudly. She couldn't wait to get to her room, strip off her clothes and sleep.

She could practically feel the weight of the sheets on her aching body.

And then, just like that, she couldn't.

Because as Willa pushed into her room (it was still her room, wasn't it?), there she was, standing right in the middle as if she owned the place. The Twig. She was back, of course.

9

Don't get mad. Get Glad.
—*Glad Trash Bags Slogan*

What sort of psycho wears wool in this heat?

As Willa Pogue charged across her bedroom, a bright pink and yellow blur laden with shopping bags from a store Laura only dreamed of shopping at—minimum price for a T-shirt was around seventy dollars—Laura knew she should be mounting some sort of counteroffensive. But the girl's outfit was so bizarre, Laura suffered a momentary brain freeze.

Willa Pogue was wearing a cable-knit sweater and long wool pants. In the summer. Not to mention the fact that she looked weird. Not just hot, but strange. The clothing stretched across her body but then seemed to hover, refusing to settle in. It was almost as if the wool didn't like her. Or maybe Willa was the one who was doing the rejecting.

Either way, just looking at Willa made Laura feel uncomfortable. Uncomfortable and sweaty.

She opened her mouth to speak but nothing came out.

Unfortunately, Willa was experiencing no such difficulties.

"Why are you in here?" she spat. "What *is* it with you and my room?"

For the first time, Laura wondered if the girl really was in-sane. It would explain a lot: the weird throw pillows, her wild outbursts and why she was dressed for the tundra in June. It would also explain why Laura hadn't been fired.

No matter. After her explosion yesterday, Laura had sworn never to fight with an employer again. It simply wasn't worth the stress. Tearing her eyes away from Willa's pants (*were they lined? If so, the girl must be melting*), she forced her voice into a neutral tone.

"I'm just cleaning. It's my job." She'd been working nonstop for what seemed like years and the room was still a mess. "I mean, you have to admit, this place is a disaster."

Willa looked around. Her eyes wandered over to the bed. Laura had placed the sheets and duvet on top but it wasn't made yet.

Laura walked over to the nightstand. She knew this next subject wasn't going to go over well but it had to be raised. She'd been cleaning homes for too many years to let it slide and be-sides, Psycho Willa already hated her, so what did it matter?

She cleared her throat. "You know, you really shouldn't leave open bags of food in your room." She lifted a bag of sour cream and onion chips as evidence. (*Grease stains on white sheets were so stubborn, but a Clorox-and-salt mixture works wonders.*) "I mean, you really shouldn't bring food into your room at all, even if it isn't—"

"Just shut *up!*" Willa scooped a throw pillow off the floor—a cupcake with the words DO YOU REALLY NEED IT? stitched across the front—and hurled it in Laura's direction.

Both girls watched in silence as the cushion cut a light, sloppy lob through the air and sailed out of a screenless window

Laura had opened to offset the cleanser scent. Laura ran toward the ledge.

The stuffed pastry had landed in a rosebush. "It's okay," she said. "It just fell onto the—"

"Don't worry about it." Willa Pogue sat down on the bed. "Throwing pillows out of windows seems to be the only thing that's really working for me lately."

"So, do you want me to run down and get that?" Laura asked uncertainly.

"Nah, one of the gardeners will find it and bring it in."

The two girls sat in silence for a minute. Laura steeled herself as she waited for Willa to remember her fury.

"They're awful, right?" Willa said. Her voice sounded distant. She grabbed the YOU CAN NEVER BE TOO RICH OR TOO THIN pillow from the floor and frowned. "It's my mother. She's always got some new idea to help me lose weight. She buys these hideous things by the boatload. I don't even read them anymore. . . ."

Laura had no idea what to say. Was Willa actually looking for sympathy?

Willa looked up. "I'm sorry I yelled at you yesterday." Her voice was softer now. "I was having a bad day." She smiled sadly. "Actually, it's more like a bad couple of years."

"No, it was my fault," Laura said. "I shouldn't have been snooping. It was, well . . . I saw your picture and we look so much alike. I was just curious."

Willa tilted her head to one side. "It's weird, isn't it? It's just, you're so . . . ." She shrugged as her voice trailed off.

"It's okay," Laura said. "And thanks for not getting me fired. After our fight—I mean, I know you could've told Emory . . ."

Willa made a sound—somewhere between a choke and a giggle—then cleared her throat. "Look, I was totally out of line." She leaned back on the bare bed and gazed up at the ceiling. "I really wasn't even all that mad you were looking through my stuff. It's just my yearbooks are kind of embarrassing. I mean, I'm not sure if you noticed or anything, but I'm not exactly student council material."

"Neither was I," Laura heard herself say. The words seemed to pop out of her mouth. "I never even went to homecoming. Not once." Until now, she'd never even known that she'd wanted to.

She glanced at Willa, wondering if she'd shared too much. The girl's emerald gaze was interested, so Laura relaxed.

"Why not?"

"McKinley job," she replied mechanically, then laughed. "Sorry, like you know what that means, right? I had to work, that's all. I was cleaning a house."

Willa's eyes widened. "Really? That's awful."

"I guess," Laura said lightly. The last thing she needed was pity from a Pogue. "But my high school was so huge, I always felt kind of invisible there." This was, after all, true. "And I was never really into sports or dances. Even if I'd been there, I really wouldn't have been there."

Willa propped herself up on one elbow. "I can relate," she said. And from the look on her face, Laura knew that she could.

Willa opened her mouth, then closed it. She sat up and stared at the fluorescent pink shopping bags scattered around the bed.

"My parents are leaving for Newport tomorrow morning without me," she blurted out, still gazing at the bags.

Laura looked at her. "I know," she said. "Emory told me when he assigned me to your room. I'm sorry."

"It's okay. Newport sucks, anyway." Willa ran a hand through her long, tousled hair. "Hey, what's your name anyway?"

"Laura Melon."

Willa swept her arm around the room. "Well, Laura, you were right. This place is kind of a pit. I'm sorry you got the shaft."

Laura shrugged. She'd actually been thinking the exact same thing just a few hours ago. Her eyes rested on the last boarding school trunk. She hadn't been able to muster the energy to open it yet. Willa followed her gaze.

"That one's the neatest, I swear."

"Listen," Laura said, suddenly all business. "I'll make you a deal—you like to sleep late, right?"

Willa's eyes narrowed slightly. "Yeah," she said slowly.

"Good. Okay, I promise not to run the vacuum until eleven AM if you promise to do the bare minimum in here . . . like no open food containers and cap all your bottles if you're packing them?"

Willa smiled. It was a familiar smile—wide and bright—and Laura suddenly realized that it was the perfect match to her own.

"Deal," Willa said.

"Great. I should get started." Laura pointed to the cleaning caddy.

Willa stretched her hands high over her head. "I gotta change before I sweat to death."

"I was wondering about that. Why did—"

Willa groaned. "Trust me, you really don't want to know."

58

She paused. "You know what? I just realized that I met your mom yesterday. She works here too, right?"

Laura nodded.

"She's great. You're really lucky." Willa's voice was touched with sadness.

Suddenly, Laura felt as if she were viewing the girl from a completely different angle. The spoiled, shrill heiress from yesterday floated up and out of the room. In her place sat a lonely, friendless girl in an ugly sweater and wool pants, hiding from the world—and herself—while her cold, hypercritical parents vacationed in an entirely different house, in an entirely different state.

Laura remembered her mother's words:

I got the feeling she isn't very happy.

Okay. So maybe a little sympathy was in order.

She turned to Willa. "I have an idea," she said.

That afternoon, Laura and Willa boxed up every last throw pillow to prepare them for their new home: the Salvation Army.

10

The world of the debutante is highly exclusive and select. Not just anyone can gain access.
—*Bibb Porter's Guide to Debutante Deportment*

"Hi, Willa, this is Caleb Blake. . . . Maybe you didn't get my, uh, other messages since it's summer and all, but, um, our parents are friends and since I guess we'll both be at Fenwick together, our moms—"

Willa leapt toward the answering machine and stabbed the Delete button.

"Talk about not getting the message," she muttered as her finger pounded away. *Delete. Delete. Delete.* The movement felt oddly soothing and she couldn't seem to stop. "How about this: *quit calling me.*"

She frowned, her hand finally dropping to her side as worry rippled through her. The Blake kid was definitely going to rat her out, and then her mother would be furious.

Whatever. She couldn't deal. Besides, it was her birthday. She shouldn't have to be hassled on her birthday, should she?

Willa's eyes landed on the engraved invitation that leaned

against her bureau. Who was she kidding? Her day was going to suck. Caleb Blake was the least of her problems.

Calm down, she ordered. *One step at a time.*

First of all, she had to find a dress. Something normal. A tall order since everything she owned made her look like a giant piece of saltwater taffy.

Okay. Maybe a little music would help. Willa carried her Mac into the dressing room and fiddled with the volume. The tiny room vibrated to the bass line of Lubé Special's "Happy Birthday, Willa." She'd woken to find the song waiting for her and had already listened to it twelve times.

Happy birthday, Willa. Happy birthday to you!

The music was just too good for reality. As the song progressed, the engraved invitation was forgotten. Willa was no longer in her dressing room; she wasn't even in Connecticut. Digging her bare toes into the carpet, she moved her body to the beat, stabbing her head up and down and side to side.

"Um, why are you head-banging in your closet?"

She spun around. Laura was in the doorway, smiling. After six weeks, Willa felt pretty comfortable in front of her new friend. But turning her dressing room into an audition for *American Idol* was definitely pushing it.

Bending at the hip, Laura began to collect the discarded clothing and a few candy wrappers.

Willa frowned as she turned off the music. She really had been nervous, she realized. She couldn't even remember *eating* Tootsie Rolls.

"Sorry it's such a mess. . . . I was just . . . I was blowing off some steam." As she spoke she could feel her anxiety returning, full force. "I have to go to Café Pertutti for this lame Fenwick meet-and-greet lunch for new students. I didn't even know it was today, but my mom FedEx'd the invite and then just called to let me know that she and my dad bagged, so now I have to go alone." The words poured out of Willa's mouth. "It's even worse that it's today 'cause it's my birthday—which my mom barely acknow—"

"Wait, sorry, did you say today was your birthday?" Laura stood up.

"Yeah. Didn't you hear the song?"

"I couldn't understand what he was saying." Despite Willa's many attempts, Laura hadn't become much of a Lubé Special fan. Laura looked at her, her face pale. "It's my birthday today, too," she said.

"How old are you?"

"Seventeen. I graduated a year early."

Willa stared at her. "Me too. Well, about the seventeen part. Obviously the graduating early thing didn't happen," she said. A laugh rose in her throat. "I guess you could say I'm taking the scenic tour."

Laura plucked a few candy wrappers off the ottoman and sat down. "Isn't that a little weird?" she said. "I mean, we look pretty much identical *and* we were born on the exact same day? What are the odds?"

The wheels in Willa's head began to churn. "Hey, maybe we *were* switched at birth! That would explain why I suck so bad at being in my family."

Laura laughed. "I wish—but I doubt you were born at the

Mediplex down on Union. My mom always jokes that she'd have received better care at the Cineplex."

Okay. So a mix-up wasn't likely, Willa thought.

Willa knew that her mother had occupied her own suite at the Darien Center for Women's Health. She'd also had a fleet of private attendants at her beck and call.

Her blood was one hundred percent Welles-Pogue.

Laura stood. "Listen, I know we're totally freaking out and everything, but I don't want to make you late."

Willa didn't speak. A plan was unfolding in her head as smoothly as a Fruit Roll-Up.

"How bad can it be?" Laura's voice was bright and coaxing. "Sure, it might not be your dream birthday or anything, but at least it's at Café Pertutti so you know the food'll be good." She laughed. "Hey, I'm jealous."

Willa never meant to be manipulative. Laura was the one who'd misinterpreted her silence as dread. Willa herself hadn't even made so much as a weepy face. Still, it was the perfect in. She couldn't resist.

"I think you should go for me," she said. It was the most Pogue-like thing Willa had ever done in her entire life.

"What?"

Now it was Willa's turn to be cheerful and convincing.

"It's just, well, I had the best idea! It's so simple—you can go in my place. For me. Get it?"

"But I wasn't invited. I won't get in."

"*Laura Melon* can't get in. But nobody there knows you're Laura Melon. You could be Willa Pogue—you know, just for today—this afternoon."

Laura blinked back at her. "You're kidding, right?"

"No, not at all. I think you'd have a great time, and I think I would too. With MySpace. I haven't even had a chance to thank Lubé for my song. Plus, I want to work on my site. You know, rearrange some things."

"Okay, first of all, the whole thing is just wrong—dishonest and wrong. Second of all, even if I did do this—which I never would—but if I did, and I got caught, I could get into some serious trouble. *And* I'd take my mom down with me."

Laura turned to leave, but Willa closed the short distance between them.

"Look, don't worry about getting caught, 'cause it won't happen," she said. Even to her own ears, her voice sounded strangely confident. "Nobody at Fenwick has ever met me and even if they had, it wouldn't matter. We look exactly alike, right?"

Willa broke off as she considered Laura's trim figure.

"Except for the weight thing, but I don't think that's a big deal, do you? It's just a few pounds."

Laura sent her a stern look. "Okay, stop. You look fine."

Willa shrugged. "I'm not saying I don't. I'm just saying that I might need a way to explain the difference between these"— she grabbed her hips—"and that." She swept her hand over what was meant to be Laura's overall thinness.

"You won't need to explain anything because this isn't happening."

Willa pouted. "You know, I'm trying to do you a favor here."

Laura laughed. "No you're not! You just don't want to go to this lunch!"

"That's true." Willa paused. "But, Laura, don't you think you deserve a break—especially on your birthday?" Willa realized she meant it. "*I* think you do. It'll be fun to pretend you're someone else—just for a few hours. You said yourself that the restaurant is supposed to be great. What possible downside is there?"

Laura hesitated. "But what about my cleaning schedule?"

"You're going to Greenwich, not Tibet. How badly can you fall behind in one day? Come on." Willa frowned suddenly as she pushed her face into Laura's. Their noses were practically touching. "Hey, are you wearing *makeup?*"

Laura took a step back and gave her head a quick, firm shake. "Wait. What?"

Willa sighed. Wasn't Laura supposed to be smart? Why was she acting so dense all of a sudden? "Makeup," she said slowly. "You're wearing makeup, right?"

"Yeah, what's wrong with that?"

"No, nothing. I just never noticed that you wore it before." She nodded firmly. "It's gotta come off."

"*Why?*"

"Willa Pogue lesson number one: I almost never wear makeup. Don't even know how to put the junk on. I just think we might as well do this right. Just to be safe." She pointed at Laura's ponytail. "And you have to wear your hair down. I never pull mine back." She studied Laura's face again. "Do you wear eyeshadow, too?"

"Ew! No! Are you kidding?" Laura wrinkled her nose. "But wait. Stop!" She raised her hand in the air. "I can't do this, Willa. Sorry. It's just—I have to pack you up for school and there's all this other . . ."

"Fine. How about I clean for you while you're gone?"

Laura laughed. "Oh, that's funny."

Willa folded her arms across her chest. She was actually a little hurt. "What's the big deal? I'll slip into a uniform and vacuum for a few hours. It won't kill me."

"Wait. You're serious?" Laura raised her eyebrows. "Forget it. Someone would definitely recognize you. Besides, you're a slob. Absolutely not. No way."

But Willa was already mopping up spills with the Brawny Man. She was taking the Lemon Pledge. She was feeling the magic of Clorox 2. . . .

She was so lost in thought that she didn't even hear the knock.

And then it got louder.

Laura shot her a look. "Do you think they heard?" she whispered.

"I don't know." Willa stared at the door as it swung open. Laura's mother stepped into the room.

"Hi, girls," she said, smiling.

She looked way too happy to have heard their conversation. In fact, she looked completely elated. Willa noticed it immediately. Andy was always in a good mood, but today she was practically floating.

"Sorry to disturb you, but I just wanted to let Laura know that we're having a guest for dinner." Her smile widened.

"You weren't disturbing me. Come in anytime," Willa said. She glanced over at Laura and frowned.

Something was wrong.

Bit by bit, the color was draining from Laura's face.

"What is it?" she whispered.

Laura shook her head. She turned to her mother. "Um, who's coming over?" There was an edge to her voice.

"I thought it might be nice for you to meet Dr. Pool—Benji. He's so eager to meet you and he doesn't have much free time, since summer's his busy season." She looked at Laura's face and her cheer seemed to falter a bit. "It's just that it would be nice for the two of you—"

"Sure. That sounds great." Laura's voice sounded tight and forced.

Her mother's face lit up. "Oh, I'm so glad. He'll be over right after work and we'll celebrate then. This is going to be so much fun." She closed the door behind her as she left.

Laura's face now matched the bottle of bleach that dangled from her cleaning caddy.

"Are you okay?" Willa asked.

Laura shook her head, as if waking herself from a trance. "I'm sorry. Dr. Pool is my mom's new boyfriend. I just didn't know how serious they were. Until now."

Willa studied her face. "Your mom looks happy," she pointed out.

Laura turned to stare at her. "Yeah, I guess," she said.

"Listen, are you sure you're okay?"

"I am. Definitely." Laura studied her hands for a second. When she looked up, her face seemed harder. Not angry, but determined. "Listen, I think maybe I will take you up on that lunch offer. If it's okay with you."

Willa blinked. "Are you sure?"

"Yeah. That was just a serious dose of reality." Laura laughed.

"And I still have to meet the guy. Maybe if I relax this afternoon I'll be in better shape tonight. But right now, I really don't want to think about it. You know what? I feel better already," Laura said. "I really need a break." She spoke this last part so softly that Willa had to crane her neck to hear.

"I'll call you a car," Willa said. "The reception starts in forty minutes."

She moved toward the door, carpet crunching under her feet. As her hand reached out for the knob she paused. "Hey, Laura?"

"Yeah?"

"Thanks." Then Willa pointed toward her gigantic closet. "Time to go shopping."

11

Sparkling Shine
—Palmolive Dishwasher Gel, Label Copy (bottle)

From the doorway at Café Pertutti, Laura observed the sea of bobbing heads as they moved up, down and around the dining room. She leaned against a coatrack, closed her eyes and channeled every ounce of her energy into not vomiting.

How had she gotten herself into this mess?

It had all happened so fast. One minute Laura was protesting the absurdity of Willa's proposal, the next she was getting into a Lincoln Town Car and answering to the name Willa Pogue.

No wonder she felt nauseous.

Laura glanced down at the outfit she'd borrowed from Willa—a green linen skirt, white peasant blouse and soft leather sandals. She'd been uncomfortable with the loan, but the situation had been urgent. She couldn't wear her uniform to the luncheon and, besides, Willa had insisted.

"I've got twenty more skirts just like it," she'd snorted. "My mom fails to accept that all I really want to wear are sweats."

The expensive clothing made Laura look even more like

Willa Pogue. The transformation had been the final, bizarre step in what had become a freakishly strange day.

After snagging a cleaning uniform from the third floor, Willa had returned to her room. Laura watched her friend move toward her as if she were watching a movie of herself. The two girls had stared at one another, paralyzed by their twin-ness.

Finally, Willa had broken the silence.

"Hey, Willa Pogue," she'd said. "I'm Laura Melon."

Laura realized her mouth was hanging open. She'd closed it and cleared her throat. "Wow," she'd replied. "Tell me about it." They reminded her of a balanced equation. Anything had seemed possible.

The problem was, Laura realized now, she and Willa weren't *really* twins. They were *pseudo*-twins. They were wannabes.

Fingering the rich cotton of her peasant blouse, Laura sighed. The outfit was, by far, the nicest she'd ever worn, but she knew she couldn't keep it. She shouldn't even be wearing it now. Add that to the long list of mistakes she'd made today. Borrowing *anything* white was dangerous. Almost as dangerous as the switch itself. What had she been thinking? She'd washed a million whites over the years (*always line dry in the sun—it's like natural Clorox*) and they were impossible to preserve. And linen wrinkled so easily (*handwash with plenty of water and pure soap. Rinse thoroughly and dry in a terry-cloth towel*). She'd spend an hour laundering this ensemble before returning it to Willa.

Oh well. It served Laura right.

I shouldn't be here, she thought, a cold sweat breaking out over her neck and forehead. *I shouldn't have let the Dr. Pool thing freak me out so much. I have to—*

"Excuse me, miss?"

A man was standing next to her. He seemed to have appeared out of nowhere, and Laura started to feel a little spooked until she remembered she was hovering in the doorway.

"Are you here for the Fenwick meet and greet?"

All she had to do was say no and everything would go back to normal. No. *Non. Nyet. Nein.*

Laura waited for her cheeks to turn their usual color, but as the seconds ticked by she felt an unfamiliar calm settle over her. She ran her hand over Willa's soft, thick linen skirt. Her feet, cradled in the fine leather sandals, suddenly improved her posture: her shoulders straightened, her chin rose.

"Actually, I am." Her voice was smooth and confident—and completely unrecognizable. "I'm just a little late. I'm so sorry."

"No problem. I got lost trying to find this place myself. I'm Mr. Stade." The man extended his hand. He looked like a nice guy, Laura decided, the kind of man she would have chosen for her mother. Forty-something, with a face as round as a tennis ball, mossy brown hair, and glasses.

"Willa Pogue," Laura said carefully, accepting his hand. She was amazed by her newfound poise. Laura Melon would have fainted by now.

"Ahh . . . Willa. You'll be a junior, right? I hope you'll consider taking my U.S. history course this semester."

They moved toward the dining room, past a huge glossy poster that read WELCOME TO FENWICK. Laura knew she should speak as little as possible. She was tightrope walking without a rope or a safety net—and she'd just pushed away her last escape ladder.

But Mr. Stade had struck a chord. Due to budget cuts, her high school's football coach had doubled as a history teacher. His entire team—and a few other jocks—had enrolled in his class looking for an easy A. Laura's homework assignments had consisted of watching ESPN Classics, then writing essays on topics such as "Should O. J. Simpson have been granted diplomatic immunity?" When she complained, the football coach had fiercely defended his curriculum, claiming that football *was* America; that he treated every class as if it were the Super Bowl.

Laura couldn't help herself.

"How is your class organized?" she asked. "Is it a chronological study?"

"Yes, but it's really much more than that." Mr. Stade's eyes were sparkling now, and Laura was suddenly glad she'd asked the question. "The course encourages students to analyze history on many levels—political, constitutional, economic, cultural—" He stopped, his eyebrows rising slightly. "Are you interested in history, Willa?"

Laura could see that Mr. Stade was surprised. Of course he was surprised—by her questions; by her responsiveness; by everything. She'd been speaking as herself, not Willa. She had to be more careful or someone was going to get suspicious. Mr. Stade was probably familiar with Willa's transcript. And Laura was guessing it didn't exactly scream model historian.

"Um, well, I never was before, but I watched a documentary this summer about the New Deal and it kind of got me interested," she lied, knowing that Willa would never, ever watch a documentary unless it was about Lubé Special. She held her breath and watched those eyebrows for a reaction.

Mr. Stade's features evened out as his mouth curved into a smile. Laura joined him. The relief that splashed over her was so intense she stifled a giggle.

"Well, if you're interested in the New Deal you'll be happy to know that we spend almost three weeks this fall focused specifically . . ."

Mr. Stade was off and running. And Laura was jogging right beside him. She exhaled deeply, feeling her body uncurl a bit more as her breath pushed out into the room—and with it, the rest of her anxiety.

Willa was right, she thought. *I do need a vacation from myself.*

And, just like that, Laura Melon let go of Laura Melon.

Moving toward the buffet, Laura approached a group of new students and introduced herself. The real Laura would never have had the guts, but Laura-as-Willa felt confident and charming.

"Where did you transfer from?" asked a short redhead named Anders. He claimed to be a sophomore but Laura found it hard to believe that he was even in high school.

Laura straightened slightly as the word rolled off her tongue. "Shipley."

"I applied there too," he said.

"Fenwick's better," interjected a skinny blond girl whose nametag read, HI, MY NAME IS HEIDI! "My sister's a senior and she loves it. She said people aren't nearly as happy at Shipley."

Laura believed it. From what she'd heard so far, Fenwick sounded amazing. How could anyone not be happy there?

The group was staring at her expectantly and Laura suddenly realized that they were waiting for her to respond. It was yet another situation in which Laura Melon would have been shaken but Laura-as-Willa wasn't fazed a bit.

"Well," she said slowly. "Shipley wasn't a good fit for me. But I don't think you can condemn a school based on one student's experience."

"Oh, definitely," Heidi agreed. "You're so right. I was just saying that there are just overall, you know, criteria . . ."

The luncheon zipped by much too quickly. One minute, Laura was Willa Pogue, eating petits fours and sipping Perrier, flanked by members of the Fenwick staff and chatty new students. The future stretched before her, manicured and lush. The next minute, she was in the car, speeding back to her old life. And back to her real future.

Laura leaned her head against the window and stared up at the bright, cloudless sky. One thing was certain. Fenwick Academy was paradise. It was Eden before that unfortunate fruit incident. The teachers were friendly and interesting, the students intelligent and enthusiastic.

And Laura desperately—with a pain she could almost reach out and touch—wanted to be a part of it.

12

The parties, the dresses, the escorts . . .
I just loved being a debutante, didn't you?
I wouldn't trade the experience
for anything.
—*Quimby Hubbard, Debutante*


```
boardgirl: ever want 2 b someone else?
lubespecial: no
boardgirl: y not?
lubespecial: if i wuz someone else i
cldnt talk 2 u
```

13

The man that's always there for you is always here.
—Brawny Paper Towels Brawny Man Ad

For a second, right before Laura turned on the light inside her front door, a glimmer of hope shot through her. It was silly, she knew. But for just a minute, in the darkness, it seemed possible that maybe, just maybe, she might be standing in the opulent marble entryway of Pogue Hall.

And everything—from now on—would be different.

Suddenly, the lights flickered. Harsh white light swept across the hallway and into Laura's eyes.

"Honey! I thought that was you!" Laura's mother appeared. Beside her stood a short, deeply tanned man.

Laura looked around the time-worn living room. Her spirit felt cleaved; stripped down to its lining.

But feeling depressed at the sight of her own apartment only made her feel worse; guilty and mean-spirited. Besides, her mother looked ultracheerful, so Laura tried to perk up.

Her mother continued, a little breathless, "We were in the kitchen." She stepped aside importantly. "Laura, this is Dr. Pool."

Tan man stepped forward. "Happy birthday, Laura," he said, handing her a bouquet of daisies. His bronze cheeks were tinged with pink. "Your mother told me you liked these."

"Thanks." Laura could feel her own cheeks coloring. She stared into the arrangement and forced herself to rise above her own discomfort. It was a sweet gesture. It was a little sad that her mom's boyfriend was the first guy to give her flowers, but that wasn't his fault.

Dr. Pool grabbed her mother's hand. "Your mother's an amazing woman," he said as the object of his affection looked on, blushing like a love-struck teenager.

Laura stood there, feeling completely lame. *How do you respond to something like that?*

But her mother and Dr. Pool were staring, so she managed to squeak out another "Thanks." That seemed to do the trick.

Dr. Pool's real name was Benji. For some weird reason, Laura's mother refused to call her new love by his first name. Instead she called him Dr. Pool—as if the guy truly held some sort of advanced degree in pool maintenance and chlorine administration.

"Isn't he just like one of those ER doctors you see on TV?" her mother whispered to her when Benji stepped out of the room to return an emergency call.

Laura stared at her.

Her mother leaned forward. "So, what do you think?"

Laura considered Dr. Pool's full effect. Her mother's eyes were wide and happy, her voice playful. She was glowing. Her mother was actually *glowing*.

Laura had heard about this sort of thing happening.

Actually, she'd seen it happen, kind of—to women on soap operas and terrible made-for-TV movies—the type of stuff she watched when she was sick and housebound. But she'd never actually thought a person could turn into a human flashlight in *real life*. And she certainly hadn't thought anything like that could ever happen to her mother—simply because she'd met a too tan man with a beeper and work boots. *That* was completely bizarre.

Laura stifled a groan. She should be supportive. That was the mature thing to do. What was wrong with her?

"Honey?"

Guilt hit Laura from all sides. Okay, so maybe it was kind of uncomfortable to watch, but Benji really did seem to love her mom. Laura remembered her mother sitting alone, all those years, watching Powerball. She'd never complained once—not about anything. Her husband had walked out on her, leaving her alone with a three-year-old daughter. And all she'd ever wanted was to make Laura happy, to provide for the two of them. Now she was asking Laura for just a little approval. It seemed like such a small thing.

Laura's throat felt tight. "Benji seems like a great guy," she said. "I'm so happy for you."

Laura's mom laughed. "It was so important to me that you like him—you know, that you approve. At my age, sweetie, you just know when you've won the Lotto." She took Laura's hand. "You know, Benji and I have been talking. It's only been six weeks and nothing's definite yet, but I don't want you to be shocked . . ."

Laura closed her eyes. She couldn't deal with any more news. "Mom, it's fine. Let's just have a good time tonight."

Her mother squeezed her hand.

"Sorry about that," Benji said, snapping his cell closed as he stepped back into the hallway. "False alarm. And Angie called on the other line. She's on her way up."

Laura's mother brightened. "Wonderful!" She turned to Laura. "Angie is Dr. Pool's daughter."

Laura jerked her head up. "Oh! Uh, great! How old is she?"

"That's the lucky part!" her mother chirped. "You're only about two years apart."

"Angie's so excited to meet you," Benji added. He turned to Laura. "She had a job out in Cornwall today so she didn't think she was going to make it, but she was able to cut out a little early."

As if on cue, the doorbell rang.

I can do this, I can do this, Laura repeated to herself.

Forcing a cheerful look on her face, she opened the door.

"Laura, this is my daughter, Ang—" Benji began.

And then Laura's feet were no longer touching the ground.

"Happy birthday to you! Happy birthday to you!" Angie boomed as she swept Laura into a bone-crushing bear hug. "It's great to meet you!"

Laura, her face buried deep in Angie's armpit, was assaulted by the stench of chlorine. Even if she'd wanted to reply she wouldn't have been able to. Her throat had closed on impact.

Please let me pass out soon, she prayed silently, her eyes tearing.

After what seemed like forever, Laura felt her feet hit the floor. Hard.

Angie shoved a finger in Laura's stricken face. "Tonight is big," she swore. "Huge."

This situation is not about me, Laura reminded herself. *And tonight is an important night for my mom. And Benji.*

Laura tried. She really did. But the rest of the evening was a catastrophe.

Once they reached the living room, Angie forced Laura to look at pictures of her boyfriend, a lifeguard at a local swimming pool.

"I fixed Glenn's swimming pool last summer—pilot needed a new starter—and it was, like, love at first sight," Angie said, pointing her beefy index finger at the photo.

Laura stared at the lifeguard, a scrawny kid covered with zinc oxide.

"He's real cute, right?" Angie demanded repeatedly as she flipped through picture after picture.

Laura couldn't help noticing that in every shot, Glenn wore the same hesitant, shaky look—and he never smiled. She wondered if maybe Angie had just yanked the kid into one of her death squeezes and the poor guy had simply been too petrified to break things off.

After the pictures, Angie dragged Laura into the parking lot to stare at her new car, a battered old Trans Am that Angie proudly introduced as Yellow Thunder.

"She's a beaut, isn't she?" Angie declared.

Up to that point, Laura had thought it was impossible to find a car in worse shape than her mother's station wagon, but

Angie had managed to do just that. Yellow Thunder looked like it had been tested for combat—and failed miserably. The door on the passenger's side had been torn off and the gaping hole was patched with a garbage bag. The mirrors were held in place with electrical tape, and there were no hubcaps.

Still, Laura nodded enthusiastically.

Big mistake.

"Hey!" Angie shrieked so loudly that Laura was sure someone in the building was going to call the police. Actually, she *hoped* someone would call the police. "Looks like you got yourself a case of the *mellow yellows*! So how about a lesson?"

"What?"

But it was too late. Angie had already popped the car's rusted hood. "Okay, you *do* know where the restrictor plate is, right?"

Laura shook her head miserably. Time had definitely stopped. She knew that now.

"Now, for Yellow Thunder it's a little different than for most cars 'cause there is none—I took it out. I got rid of the muffler, too. I like to announce my presence with authority. . . ."

By the time they were called for dinner, Laura was covered with motor oil, grease and a few burns. Slamming down the rusted hood within inches of Laura's hand, Angie had raced upstairs, where she'd eaten thirds of everything while everyone else was still serving themselves firsts.

After dessert, Angie had insisted on checking out Laura's room. Laura had opened her mouth to protest, but Angie was already gone, racing down the hall.

When Laura finally caught up with her, Angie was already rifling through her things.

"Wow, you've got an awful lot of books, you know that? Are you, like, some kind of professor or something?"

It was the first question Angie had asked about Laura's life—her own interests—the whole evening. Unless you counted the dozens of times she'd said, "Hey, how come your cheeks turn all red like that every time you talk?"

After that, Angie started calling Laura the professor. Laura repeatedly asked Angie to stop—about thirty times in all. But, not surprisingly, Angie wasn't the best listener. Laura had a feeling "the professor" would be engraved on her tombstone.

Finally, after Angie had dealt her last organ-smashing hug and lurched off into the night, Laura said good night to her mom and Benji and escaped to her room.

She lay down on the bed. Every inch of her was sore and bruised. What a day. She'd gone from heiress to Angie. It was quite a tumble.

She sighed. She loved her mother and she was happy for her. But Angie was a nightmare.

Laura's thoughts turned to Willa, sleeping soundly in her million-dollar mansion.

Envy reigned over her.

Willa had money. Willa had Fenwick. Willa had everything.

From the kitchen, Laura could hear her mother and Benji, laughing together as they filled out a Publishers Clearing House sweepstakes application.

Even if her last name wasn't Pogue, her mother had found a way to make her own life glitter.

Now Laura just had to do the same for herself.

14

The etiquette of telephoning is quite
important and many otherwise perfectly
well-bred people often make themselves
conspicuous because they do not know the
correct procedure in using this modern but
almost indispensable invention.
—*Perfect Behavior*
Donald Ogden Stewart

Willa's foot skimmed the lukewarm water as her silver raft drifted across the pool. Yesterday had been incredible.

She'd reprioritized her MySpace friends, streamed three new Lubé Special songs, logged some quality TV time, then topped it all off with a sound, dreamless sleep.

The vacation from herself had, in fact, been so fantastic that she had decided to extend it into this morning. She would reclaim her dreary life when she laid eyes on Laura Melon. Not a second sooner.

And that meant the person floating in the Pogues' heated pool did not answer to the name Willa Tierney Pogue. Her name was Laura Melon.

It would have to be. Willa Pogue avoided bare bathing suit

situations at all costs. She never hung out at the pool without the safety of some sort of towel or cover-up. *This* girl—the person she was now—felt fantastic in her black tank.

There was only one problem with this picture: the phone was ringing.

BBBBeeep. BBBBeeep.

Willa popped one eye open and turned toward the sound. "God, that's loud," she muttered. She hadn't even known there was a phone out here. She made a mental note to turn the volume down—or better yet, *off*—when she got out of the pool.

Hello, you've reached the . . .

There was a machine out here, too? That figured. God forbid her mother miss an important call from the Junior League while she was underwater.

On the plus side, at least the ringing had stopped. Hopefully, the idiot would just hang up, rather than leave a message. It was probably that loser Blake kid. Why wouldn't he just give up?

"Willa! Willa Pogue! Pick up the phone immediately! I will *not* have this particular conversation with an answering machine! Do you unde—"

Her mother's voice vibrated like a cherry bomb. Willa flipped off the raft and plunged into the water.

Her minivacation had come to a catastrophic halt.

Maybe Laura got caught, Willa considered as she swam to the side. *She never called. Maybe she's in real trou—*

"If you don't pick up this phone in the next thirty seconds, I'm sending Emory to find out exactly what it is that you've been up to down there, because—"

Willa sprinted out of the pool, upsetting a row of patio

furniture. Green and white cushions rained down around her as she grabbed the phone.

"Hi, Mom," she sputtered. "What's up?

"Don't you 'what's up' me," her mother railed. "I hate that expression. It's so coarse, Willa."

Willa stifled the urge to throw the phone in the pool. *Tell me why you're calling,* she thought. *Is Laura in trouble? Am I in trouble?*

"Sorry," she said. "Um, so, what's wrong?"

"What's wrong," her mother shot back, her voice heavy with disdain, "is that I just received a call from Fenwick. They haven't received your housing application yet. The deadline was June twenty-sixth! You also haven't submitted any essays on your summer reading. Orientation begins at the end of August, Willa. That's just over a month from now. As in *four weeks*. *What* have you been doing all summer?"

Willa ran a hand through her tangled wet hair and squeezed her eyes shut. *Four weeks.*

"Don't worry," she reassured her mother. Her tone was even and measured. "It's probably just a computer glitch. I'll take care of everything."

"You'd better take care of this, Willa Tierney. Do you hear me? Do you? Because I'm supposed to be at the Watleys' right now, playing mixed doubles. Bitsy Perkins had to step in for me at the last minute and her tennis elbow has been a problem all season. . . ."

Willa apologized to the entire Newport tennis circuit and hung up the phone. She looked down at her dripping body and grimaced. Willa Pogue was back. And so were all her hangups.

Wrapped in a huge beach towel, Willa walked across the lawn toward the house. She let herself in through the kitchen. Her damp feet slapped against the bright black and white tile, leaving a trail of sloppy wet splotches in her wake.

"Where, where," she muttered as she threw open every cabinet door in the pantry. She remembered getting some sort of large envelope from Fenwick a few weeks ago, right after she'd made a snack run to the 7-Eleven. She'd probably shoved it onto one of these shelves, along with the contraband items.

Her eyes came to rest on a large manila envelope. It was folded in half and sandwiched between a half-empty bag of Doritos and a two-liter bottle of Diet Coke.

There were a few other Fenwick envelopes behind that one.

Don't panic, she thought as she tightened her grip around the beach towel. *Four weeks is actually a really long time.*

Her stomach issued a long, low growl, reminding her that she hadn't eaten yet today.

Willa grabbed the envelopes, the Doritos and the Coke and headed back to the pool.

If I have to be myself, I might as well be myself by the pool, she reasoned.

She spread her bundle on a chaise lounge and waded through the morass of papers. After a few minutes, she heard a loud clanging sound and turned toward the driveway. Laura's ancient station wagon rolled to a stop.

"Hey! Over here!" Willa raised her hand high over her head to get Laura's attention. As she did, a few drops of water landed on her housing application, smearing the ink.

Willa frowned and rubbed at the spot. The smudge grew larger.

Laura cut across the lawn. She paused at the overturned row of furniture.

"I know, I know," Willa murmured, waving toward the heap. "My mom called and was really pissed. I have to, like, get serious about school." She fanned the papers out in front of her and shook her head. "I have to write some sort of entrance essay or something—about summer reading? I don't know, though. I think I lost that sheet. But I guess I could call the school. Or maybe do it all online." She frowned. "That really sucks, doesn't it? Well, maybe not for you, but it does for me. I hate writing papers."

When Willa was eight, she'd received a "Build Your Own Volcano" kit for Christmas, along with a note informing her that the toy was for "outside use only." She'd ignored the note, choosing instead to set up her mini–Mount St. Helens on an eighteenth-century dining room table her mother had recently purchased from an estate sale.

Willa had known the situation was going to end badly from the very start. No sooner had she poured the colored baking soda down the model's tiny neck than the volcano began to sputter and jerk. Within seconds, the thing had erupted—a fast and furious belch that coated everything in sight.

Staring at Laura now, she was suddenly reminded of her toy volcano. Her normally calm, mellow friend looked ready to erupt.

It's probably something with her mom's boyfriend, Willa

thought. She shoved some Doritos into her mouth and leaned back. *Let the lava flow.*

"Of course you hate writing papers, Willa," Laura snapped. "You hate everything. Except for this crap." She gave the Doritos bag a hard shake, triggering a maelstrom of tiny red triangles. She pointed at Willa's papers. "Look at this mess. You haven't even filled out any of these forms and they've got orange fingerprints all over them. And they're *wet.* I can't believe you."

Willa's mouth dropped open. Wait, why was Laura against her too?

Laura picked up a glossy brochure. "Do you know how amazing Fenwick is?" Her eyes narrowed. "No, wait; do you even know *where* Fenwick is?"

Willa shifted her weight uncomfortably. She had a feeling Fenwick was somewhere in Connecticut, but she wouldn't be willing to put money on that.

Laura scowled. "Of course you don't! Oh—and I had a great time at the luncheon yesterday, thanks for asking. Honestly, Willa, you're so spoiled. Don't you know how lucky you are?"

Willa felt a stray tear wander down her cheek. "Of course you think I'm lucky. You have no idea what you're talking about. Or what my life is like. You've never even met my parents—the people who you work for—have you? Well, you won't, believe me."

"That's such a rich kid's argument. Who cares that you don't see your parents that much? They obviously care about you! They send you to the best schools, buy you the best clothes; you have houses that are nicer than the ones in magazines . . . don't you know how—"

"And don't *you* know that the cheapest way to pay for any-thing is with money?"

Laura blinked. "What?"

Willa shrugged. "You heard me. Once you have money—a lot of it—the best of everything isn't that huge a sacrifice, is it?"

"I hadn't really thought about it that way."

"Of course you hadn't. You were too busy thinking about how good I've got it." She looked at Laura. "You just don't get it, do you? You've got it pretty good yourself."

Laura sat down on the foot of the chaise lounge. "How could you think my life is anything other than horrible?" she asked quietly.

Willa pulled her knees up to her chin. "I see the way you and your mom are together. You guys are a team."

"I guess. I mean, I know. My mom is great," Laura allowed. "But—and I'm not trying to be argumentative here or anything—I do spend my days scrubbing toilets. Other people's toilets. Doesn't that guarantee an instant gold medal in the my life sucks the most contest?"

"And I spend my days being a disappointment," Willa said, laughing. She wrapped her arms around her bent knees. "And just so you know, I did do a little cleaning yesterday. Not a lot, I guess, but a little. It didn't seem all that bad."

"Well, how about this new development? The magnificent Dr. Pool has a daughter. Try to imagine NASCAR meets the *WWE SmackDown* and that's Angie. *And* she's decided we're BFF. I definitely rack up some bonus points for that, don't you think?"

"No way. Angie at least *likes* you. The kids I meet at board-ing school barely even talk to me."

Laura sighed. "I'm sorry, Willa." She sank back onto her elbows and squinted into the sun. "I don't know, it's like I got drunk at that luncheon yesterday or something. Drunk on your last name. I know it's crazy, but I just kept imagining myself at Fenwick, taking classes, studying, filling out my college ap—"

"It's not crazy," Willa blurted out. Her mind was on overdrive, her hand dipping into that box of Fruit Roll-Ups again. It was all so clear. The next few months stretched before her, smooth, light and tasty.

"What? What are you talking about?" Laura said, sitting up. Her voice was tinged with worry. She'd been inside the Fruit Roll-Up box before too. She knew it was dangerous.

"Look, since you're obviously such a perfect match for Fenwick, why don't you go—as me? Just for this semester," Willa said, trying hard to contain her excitement. "Take classes, relax, get ready for college—do whatever—and I'll move into your house and take over your cleaning route."

Laura frowned. "Look, I know you don't want to go back to school. And I know you have a lot of forms to fill out, so maybe it's just the stress that's getting to you—"

Willa shook her head. "It's not the stress. Don't you get it? We already pulled this off. If nobody at the Fenwick thing suspected anything, I don't see why we'd have a problem."

"You don't, do you?" Laura said, laughing. "Willa, yesterday we switched places for three *hours*. You're proposing we switch for over four *months*."

"You say potato, I say—" Willa paused. "Wait, how does that one go?"

"Never mind. The point is, this is more complicated than

my putting on an expensive outfit and borrowing your invitation," Laura said, her voice stern. "Plus, the thought of *you* wanting to clean is a joke. You're the biggest slob I've ever met." She ended with a grand, sweeping gesture at Willa's stack of Dorito-stained papers.

"Hey! I've gotten *a lot* neater since we've met, haven't I?"

Laura didn't even bother to answer.

"Okay, fine," Willa said, trying hard not to sulk. Laura was taking the entire Fruit Roll-Up box away from her, placing it on a shelf far out of her reach, and she was desperate to stop her. "I'm messy. But anything's better than school. And I *did* clean a little bit yesterday. Plus, I've watched you. I've learned a lot."

"Yesterday doesn't count. I'm sorry, but pushing around a vacuum for a few hours isn't cleaning. This job's not as easy as it looks. Besides, in the fall people are back from vacation. My mom and I have a pretty hectic schedule."

Willa couldn't let go. She needed this. "So what? You can teach me. This'll work, Laura. I swear. We can do this, just—"

Laura groaned and raised a hand, cutting her off.

"Look, as much as I'm dreading these next few months," she said, "I just can't. I'm sorry. I hate to let you down, but I can't do this. Think about what would happen if we got caught. We'd get into so much trouble. Even worse, we'd get my mom into trouble." She shuddered. "And if that happened, I just couldn't live with myself. So let's just stop the whole 'wouldn't it be great if' thing because it's never going to work." She tightened her ponytail. "I mean, maybe you'll have a great time at school and I'll discover some sort of deep-seated love for cleaning."

"Do you honestly believe that?" Willa asked.

"No." Laura's voice was smaller now. "I honestly believe that the next few months are going to be awful. But I can't switch places with you, Willa. I'm sorry."

"That's okay," Willa said. "I understand." She meant it, too. She knew Laura was every bit as miserable as she was.

Willa stared down at her heap of forms. "I should get ready for school."

"Back to cleaning for me."

Laura pushed herself onto her feet. As she did, loose Doritos danced around on the chaise lounge.

"Don't want to mess up the patio," Willa muttered. She scooped them up and dropped them into her bitter, waiting mouth.

15

The scent is all you'll notice.
—*Renuzit Airlets*

What was that smell?

As Laura pushed open the front door her nostrils were assaulted by a stench so horrible her eyes rolled back into her head. The entire apartment reeked of burnt fur with undertones of urine, stale beer and garbage. She'd never smelled a dead person before, but instinct told her that this situation was far worse.

She'd been right to turn down Willa's offer. She'd definitely taken the moral high road.

So why was she being punished?

There was no other way to interpret the events of the past week leading up to—and including—this very pungent moment.

First of all, her mom and Benji were now engaged. This, of course, was not a bad thing. Laura liked Benji and, even though the couple hadn't yet celebrated their two-month anniversary, she wasn't the least bit surprised when it happened. For almost four straight days, her mom had been dropping the most ridiculous hints ("Keep Christmas clear! My lips are sealed, but there might just be a wedding ring underneath that mistletoe!") to prepare her for the "big news."

So when she'd returned from Blockbuster one night to find the couple sitting in the living room listening to the Cash5 drawing (they'd lost but had been too love-struck to care) with huge goofy smiles plastered across their faces, she'd known it had happened.

"Guess what?" her mother gushed. "I'm going to be Mrs. Dr. Pool! Isn't that terrific? Oh—just look at my ring! Benji splurged and bought me a diamond. Isn't it huge? You know doctors!"

Laura had done her best to feign interest. Despite the sadness she felt about her own life, she was truly happy for them.

"Angie would love to be here," Benji explained, shaking his head apologetically. "She stopped by when you were out but got called to Stamford on an emergency. She was so disappointed that she missed you."

Maybe Angie's not so bad after all, Laura thought charitably.

"She can't wait to be your stepsister. And roommate."

Suddenly, the room was spinning. The air had run cold.

Her mother shot Benji a look and asked him for a moment alone with her daughter. He kissed her cheek and stepped out of the room.

"Mom, what's going on?"

Her mother spoke softly. "Honey, I'm sorry. I know this is a lot and I wanted to explain it all myself—you know, just the two of us." She sighed. "It's true. Benji and Angie are going to move in and since there are only two bedrooms here you girls will have to share a room."

Laura dug deep, she really did. She tried to think up something—anything—positive to say about her new living situation. But she just couldn't do it.

Her mother's voice was normal—cheerful and bright—but something in her expression told Laura there was something she wasn't telling her.

"Until Christmas, the house will be all girls—just you, Angie and me. Won't that be fun?"

"Why? Where's Benji going?" Laura asked.

"Well, Benji has a brother in Miami and they'd like to open a Dr. Pool down there this winter," her mother explained. "He's leaving Angie in charge of things up here and is planning to be back by December."

"Wait. I don't understand," Laura said. "You guys are engaged and now he's just . . . leaving?"

"Benji asked me to go with him, but I told him that you and I were a team and that I just couldn't leave you. I didn't think it was fair to you, what with the business and all."

Laura opened her mouth, then closed it. "I'm sorry, Mom. I don't know what to say."

Her mother reached for Laura's hand, her engagement ring sparkling in the light. "It's fine, honey. Really. We'll talk every day and Benji's going to teach me how to use the computer so I can . . ."

Laura couldn't listen to any more. She felt too guilty. Her mother loved Benji, and she wasn't going to see him for four whole months because of her fully grown daughter? It didn't seem fair.

On the other hand, leaving Laura alone with a full cleaning roster *and* Angie hardly seemed fair either.

". . . Oh, and Benji wanted you to know," her mother was saying, "just as soon as he gets this new business up and running, he's going to really try and add money to your college account, Laura. He's not sure he'll be able to this year—for your freshman year—but he's determined to, just as soon he can. Because you're his daughter now too."

"Uh, thanks," Laura said. "That's really sweet of him."

"It is, isn't it? He's always surprising me."

A small giggle escaped her mother's lips and her hand flew up to her mouth to stifle it. And it was then that Laura understood: her mother had purposely tried to check her excitement because she didn't want that to sway Laura's thinking.

But the truth was her mother was dying to go to Florida. The giggle had said it all. It hung in the air, leaving a trail of tiny exclamation points around her mother's head.

Her mother loved Benji. Her place was with him now.

Laura ran through the fall cleaning roster. She could handle the homes by herself for a few months. It would be tedious, but she could do it.

But life with Angie? Laura had tried to picture it, but the best her stress-addled brain could conjure was an image of herself in traction.

Okay, maybe Florida wasn't such a good idea after all.

And that was when she caught sight of her mother's hand, resting in her own. That red, callused skin—a housecleaning casualty.

My mother has never taken a vacation, Laura realized.

Suddenly another vision shot through her mind: her mother, sitting in the sun, walking along the beach and buying Lotto cards at a seaside 7-Eleven.

Leaning forward, she impulsively threw her arms around her

mother's neck and kissed her cheek. "I'm so happy for you," she blurted out. Tears pearled in the corners of her eyes. "And you've got to promise to send me lots of postcards from Miami."

Her mom pulled back, confused. "But, honey—"

"Mom. For once, don't worry about Darien Full Service Home Maintenance. I can totally take care of things here, and you can be with Benji."

"Oh, Laura, I don't think—"

"Mom! It's only four months, right?"

"It's just—we've never been apart, Laura," her mom had said, biting her lip. "We've been a team, ever since you were born."

"We still will be. But it's like you said. You know when you've won the Lotto." Laura had squeezed her mom's callused hand. "And you have, Mom. For once in your life, just have fun. Eat key lime pie, wear bright clothes, rent a convertible—do whatever it is middle-aged people in Florida do. And I'll be totally okay." She'd taken a big breath. "Angie and I will be fine."

By the look on her mother's face, Laura knew she'd done the right thing. She and her mom and Benji had spent the rest of the night laughing and talking. And at the time, Laura had meant every word.

Now, however, standing in the entryway, breathing foul, possibly toxic fumes, Laura wondered if perhaps she'd overstated things.

For instance, there was obviously a broken sewage pipe somewhere in the building. That was something she really, really didn't feel up to dealing with.

But what choice did she have? Her mother was over at Benji's planning the Florida trip.

"Great," she muttered, clamping a hand over her nose.

Her life really did stink.

She dreaded calling the super—a total jerk—but she knew that her bitterness really stemmed from that Fenwick lunch and the knowledge that her fate was now sealed. Having turned down Willa's offer, Laura would never see Fenwick Academy in its fully realized, three-dimensional glory.

"What did you expect?" she asked herself. "That someone was going to show up and magically offer you a scholarship? You don't *belong* there. You already graduated from high school. And now you're talking to yourself."

The super's number was in the kitchen, taped to the refrigerator. Laura trudged down the hall, feeling increasingly sorry for herself with every step. Her apartment was broken and disgusting. She was going to have to beg the super to make an after-hours house call. He'd probably expect a tip or—

Ooph.

Laura's foot slid into something hard, sending her flying.

A purple footlocker. It had Angie written all over it. Literally. It was clearly a homemade job: manic bubble letters, strangely malformed block letters, plain, bold print and even a few failed attempts at calligraphy.

"No," Laura said. Her mouth seemed unable to form any other words. "No."

The phone rang.

Laura didn't want to answer. She wanted to run away and live in a ditch. Or under a bridge. Or even hurl herself from one.

Still holding her nose, she reached for the phone. "Hello?"

Loud static shot through her ear, so piercing that Laura almost dropped the receiver. She frowned and rubbed her head.

"Ow, I mean, hello?" she repeated.

"Professor! How are you?"

"Hi, Angie," she said weakly. "I'm fine. How are you?"

"Great! I keep trying to swing by but summers are crazy for Dad and me. People freak out if they can't go swimming, you know?"

"I'll bet." Laura checked her watch. She really hoped Angie wouldn't talk for long. She had to get a handle on the plumbing situation.

"Anyway," Angie said, "I was just calling about the rug. Isn't it great?"

"Rug?" Laura asked.

"Aw, did I ruin the surprise? I know we're not, like, official roomies for another month but I saw it and thought it'd be perfect so I was like, hey, why not start decorating now? I put it in your room. . . ."

Laura's mouth fell open.

"No," she whispered. "No."

"I meant to move my trunk too, but then I got beeped. . . ."

Laura leaned against the wall and pinched the bridge of her nose. She'd never had a migraine before, but she was sure a massive one was about to hit and she wanted to be prepared.

"And I burned you a CD—kind of like a belated birthday gift. It's in your room, too."

"Thanks, Angie. That's, um, really sweet."

"I'm just sorry it's late. But I'll make it up to you. We'll have lots more birthdays together, right? Listen, I'm driving into a tunnel so I better—"

She was gone, in a blaze of crackling feedback.

Laura hung up the phone and walked to her room. When she reached her doorway, she nudged the door open with her foot and winced as the smell of decaying trash hit her full force.

There it was.

Stretched out across the floor was the rattiest rug Laura had ever seen. It was supposed to be zebra skin but was so filthy that the white stripes were almost as dark as the black. In many spots the fur had been completely rubbed off. And, of course, the odor was unbearable.

"Why is this happening to me?" Laura wailed.

The CD was on top of the rug. The cover featured a picture of Angie sitting in Yellow Thunder, wearing yellow shades and flashing the peace sign. She'd named the mix *The Professor's Got Yellow Fever.*

Was it possible that Angie had actually never heard of the yellow fever virus?

Actually, the name is weirdly fitting, Laura thought. *At this very moment, I'm probably contracting some entirely new, disgusting disease that's passed only through low-quality animal prints.*

Laura was a practical girl. She was thoughtful and disciplined. She never grabbed more than one napkin from a dispenser and only shopped during sales. She reused Ziploc bags *and* wrapping paper. In kitchens, her favorite cabinet was the silverware drawer, with its neat lines and subdivisions. Order ruled her life. Common sense guided her every move.

And it was sheer common sense that was speaking to her

now—*shouting*, in fact—telling her that life with Angie was a practical impossibility.

I can't do it, she thought, staring at the rug. *Angie's not even here yet and I can't take it. And there's no real, honest way out, either. If I tell my mom or Benji the truth they'll be crushed. But if I tell Angie the truth, well, she'll be crushed too, I guess. Or she'll crush me. She'll crush me even if I don't hurt her feelings.*

Laura sighed. Willa was right. It was risky, but it just might work.

Slowly, with her usual care and attention, she dressed herself in Willa's clothing—the clothing she'd been too furious to return after the luncheon.

Ten minutes later Laura was gliding into Willa's room.

"Hi," she said. "I'm Willa Pogue."

Willa was sitting on her bed. She shoved the rest of a Pop-Tart into her mouth, stretched her arms high over her head and smiled.

"You rich kids sure do like to make an entrance."

16

*The ball may only last for one night but
being a debutante is most certainly
a forever thing.*
—Rules for Debutantes
Lacey Chandler

Willa opened her eyes and stared at her alarm clock.

One minute. She only had to be herself for one more minute.

"Why wait?" she asked the darkness of her room, leaning over to click off the alarm. She hopped out of bed and dressed quickly. She felt like she was floating and gave her head a hard shake—a reminder that she wasn't dreaming.

It was August twenty-sixth: move-in day at Fenwick Academy. For all boarding school students, move-in symbolized the death of summer. Sure, classes wouldn't start up for another few days—there was always the prerequisite stream of boring assemblies and picnics—but vacation was essentially over. It was back to bondage, a return to the monotony of schedules and the pack mentality. . . .

Except this year, Willa's move-in day meant something else entirely: no more tests; no more snooty kids; no more disappointed teachers. Not for the next few months at least.

She was *free*.

Willa grabbed her bags and padded down the dark hallway. When she reached the top of the staircase, she leaned forward slightly and considered the grand floor beneath her. The over-sized chandeliers flickered in the morning sun, but somehow— even in the light—the polished marble still looked onyx.

She'd be cleaning those floors tomorrow, Willa realized, a strange excitement spreading over her.

She pressed her full weight against the banister and lifted her feet off the ground.

She'd left the mansion a million times, but today felt different. Today her stomach wasn't lined with dread.

And, of course, she'd be back tomorrow.

But tomorrow she'd be Laura Melon.

Lowering herself onto the carpet, Willa scanned the luxurious expanse of her childhood home. "You won't tell, right?" she whispered conspiratorially.

When the station wagon rolled into the driveway at six-fifteen, Willa was waiting by the kitchen door. She tossed her bags into the backseat, then silently followed Laura into the mudroom, where the trunks and suitcases were packed and waiting for Laura's Fenwick sojourn. They loaded them into the back of the car, then slid into the front seat.

"Did anyone see you upstairs?" Laura probed.

Willa tried to send her a withering look, but it was dark and Laura's head was lowered over her seat belt. "It's six in the morning. Who would've seen me?"

"I don't know. Someone. It only takes one witness, you know."

"Calm down," Willa said. Her yawn stretched into a grin. "It's not like I was walking through the house with a sawed-off shotgun. I was carrying a duffel bag on the morning before school. Even if someone did see me—which they didn't—why would they be suspicious?"

Laura drove the car down the long circular driveway toward the street. "I don't know. They wouldn't, I guess. Sorry, I'm just nervous."

"Why? Everything's gone smoothly so far."

It was true. Laura had finished her summer reading, filled out her housing application and packed without a hitch. Nobody at Fenwick had even blinked.

Laura checked the rearview mirror. Her voice was still tense. "I think maybe that's why. It just seems too easy."

"If you're really gonna be me until Christmas you've gotta try and relax," Willa said, shaking her head. She looked out her window, at the shadowy trees and black houses. "Let's go over the rules again. It'll make you feel better."

"Good idea," Laura said, visibly perking up at the thought of doing something constructive. "Okay. We can't contact one another at all, unless it's an emergency."

"Right." Laura didn't own a cell phone, and e-mail and IMs were way too risky. Willa had heard stories about boarding school administrations routinely invading student accounts in search of honor code violations.

"And you'll take a breather from MySpace and will text Lubé in private." Laura shot a stern look down the length of the dashboard. "And you *won't* tell him about the plan."

"Right. No problem. He'll be starting school again anyway so his days'll be pretty full."

Laura's mouth twitched. "Are you *sure* you can cut down on your Lubé habit?" she teased.

"What's *that* supposed to mean?" Willa snapped, sounding more defensive than she'd intended.

Laura laughed. "Wow! Okay, forget I said anything." She stuck her hand out the window to signal for a turn. "It's just, you two seem pretty hooked on each other, that's all."

Willa wrapped the seat belt around her wrist and pulled a sour face. "Hooked? Who says hooked?" She studied her feet. "I don't even know the guy's real name, Laura."

"All right. Fine. Just make sure you hide your phone and follow the rule about, you know—"

"I will, I will." Willa turned back to Laura, eager to change the subject. "So, how about you?"

"What about me?"

"You can't make friends. Even if you meet someone you like, it's just not worth it. You might let your guard down or something."

"I keep telling you that one won't be a problem," Laura countered. "I'm really not the 'it' girl type. It's my dishpan hands, I think."

"You won't even be tempted, believe me." Willa's voice was heavy and bitter. "Boarding school kids are total jerks."

Laura's eyes narrowed slightly. "And when Caleb Blake shows up I'll say hello, apologize for not returning his calls, and you really think that'll be the end of it?"

Willa leaned her head against the seat and scowled. Caleb Blake had left *another* message yesterday afternoon. Whatever his college plans were, they should seriously include a major in stalking—or some intensive therapy. "Definitely. I guarantee he'll be horrible. Everyone my parents know is. He'll want to ditch you as fast as possible, so no worries there."

"Fine." Laura stopped the car at a light and smoothed her hair with her hand. "All right, here's another one: What do you do when my mom calls the apartment?"

"Talk as little as possible. You'll be calling her from Fenwick every four days."

"Right." Laura hesitated. "Listen, are you sure your parents aren't going to try to call or visit or something?"

Willa shook her head firmly. "I told you. They only call when I've done something wrong. Keep your grades up and all you'll get are a few lame care packages. Next question."

"Okay, okay. How about cleaning—what's the best way to get water stains off bathroom fixtures?"

"Baking soda and vinegar, ma'am," Willa recited. She tossed in a little salute for good measure.

"Great." Laura lowered her voice a peg. "And what's *the* most important rule to remember when you're cleaning?"

Willa cleared her throat and screwed her eyes shut. "Um, let's see . . . that *Bounty's* the quicker picker-upper?"

"I'm serious."

"Sorry, sorry. I will never *ever* squeeze the Charmin?"

"*Willa.*"

"Fine," Willa said, thrusting her lower lip forward in a full pout. "I will speak only when spoken to."

Laura shook her head. "That's only part of it, remember? When you walk into a client's home, you're invisible only until—"

"Until *they* see me and not the other way around." Willa yawned. "I *know*."

She and Laura had both been surprised at how easily she'd memorized Laura's fall cleaning roster and other vital bits of information. But Laura kept on harping on how this was a "service-oriented field" and Willa was getting sick of it.

"Do you really?" Laura turned the car into the train station and looked at Willa, her eyes dark. "Because this is really, really important. It's a job. It's what my mom and I do to pay rent. And we can't afford to lose a single one of those houses. You *have* to be professional. You have to work hard and stay focused. No matter what."

The words bounced off the walls of the car like an echo. A *job*. She, Willa Pogue, had a job. Several, in fact.

Shame flushed through her body. She'd been so busy celebrating her own freedom that she hadn't really thought about what was at stake here. Laura was right. This was not a game.

When she'd screwed up all those other times, she'd been the only person affected.

What have I done? I've never been successful at anything in my entire life. Why should this situation be any different?

Willa looked down. Her hands were shaking slightly. "Laura, I'm not sure—"

"Yes, you are," Laura said as she pulled into a parking space and cut the ignition. Her voice was gentle but strong. "You're smart. You'll figure it out. We've gone over everything, Willa. You know this. I know you won't mess up."

"I won't," Willa repeated, tilting her head back and exhaling deeply. *I can do this.* She felt her panic melt away, like a Hershey's bar in the sun.

"So now that that's settled, I feel like I should officially welcome you to the world of the invisible," Laura said. She laughed. "It's pretty incredible, actually."

"What do you mean?" Willa frowned. Laura had given her a spiral notebook filled with homemade cleaning concoctions and secret tricks of the trade. She'd been studying it religiously, but she didn't think her brain could handle any more new information.

"It's not something you can explain. But you'll find out soon, don't worry."

The morning air felt thick against Willa's skin. She looked around the deserted parking lot and shivered. The quiet of the place was overwhelming. They'd purposely arrived two hours early so that nobody would see them together, but Willa hadn't planned on the discomfort factor.

"Do you want me to hang out a little?" she asked as she helped Laura carry her bags onto the platform.

Laura sat down on the trunk. "That's okay, thanks. You should probably get over to the apartment as soon as possible. So you're there before Angie."

Willa shifted back and forth on the balls of her feet. She wondered what a complete stranger would think of this scene. It was normal enough: two sisters—identical twins, maybe—taking a vacation.

It wasn't far from the truth.

"Have fun being me," Laura whispered.

"You too," Willa said, reaching out for Laura's hand. It was an impulsive move—completely out of character—and she was surprised by how natural it felt. As their long fingers intertwined, Laura's skin was smooth and cool against her own.

And it was impossible to tell where one girl ended and the other began.

17

Less laundry, more life
—Maytag

As the cab reached the gates of Fenwick Academy, the butterflies in Laura's stomach flew higher, tickling her throat.

"Turn here, right?" the driver shouted from around his cigar.

"Yes."

Laura peered through the window as the taxi wound its way toward the school. She resisted the urge to clap like a three-year-old.

She was in heaven.

Fenwick was even prettier than the glossy pictures in Willa's information packet. Green lawns sprawled for miles; trees swept the campus; the brick and wooden buildings dated back to the eighteenth century. Everything was perfectly maintained. And it was all huge. The library alone—a magnificent stone structure covered with columns and gargoyles—was twice the size of Laura's old high school.

When they reached her dorm, Hubbard House, Laura paid the driver but didn't go inside. She stood in front of the building and stared out at the quad, trying to lock down the moment forever. All around her, the campus buzzed with life: kids were tossing Frisbees, shouting to one another from windows, un-loading cars filled with their belongings. An unfamiliar ripple of school spirit swept through her.

She was a student here.

Sort of.

She turned and lugged her suitcases up three steps and onto the dorm's wraparound porch. She knew her room number and that she had a single—all upperclassmen did—but all other details were a mystery.

As she glanced down at the wooden beams under her feet, Laura's pulse accelerated. The rooms in this place were probably amazing, very *Pride and Prejudice*. Most of the dorms had, at one point, been private residences. She closed her eyes and pictured a slightly smaller version of Willa's bedroom at Pogue Hall. The dorm looked like it might have been built around the same time. Hopefully, there'd be a window seat looking out over the quad.

Laura opened the front door, which screeched loudly, and slid her things down the hall toward room 112. The dorm room was wide open—ready and waiting.

And completely disgusting.

The carpeting was some sort of rough Astroturf that stank of mildew—which made sense because it was slightly damp. It made Angie's filthy zebra skin seem luxurious. A single, naked lightbulb was screwed into the ceiling, encircled by a dirty ring where a fixture had once hung. There was no window seat—there was no room for one. There was barely room for the graffiti-covered desk and the flimsy metal twin bed.

Laura tilted her head sideways, then up. Wait, how could

that be? The room was slanted. Everything—bed, desk, window—sagged toward the right. Laura felt like she'd stepped inside the set of *Alice's Adventures in Wonderland*. She leaned sideways and the room instantly righted itself once again.

"I can't believe this," Laura muttered as she eyed the stained mattress (didn't *everyone* know the baking soda/peroxide trick? Honestly). "This school costs thirty-five thousand dollars a year, how do—"

She froze, horrified at her indignation. She'd been on campus for about ten minutes and already she was acting like a spoiled debutante. True, she'd read the brochures. And yes, Fenwick did cost thirty-five thousand dollars. But it wasn't *her* thirty-five thousand dollars. This—none of this—was hers. And that meant it was not hers to judge. She was in no position to make demands, either. She had to try to remember that.

It was important not to lose perspective. Again.

Besides, she was miles away from her vast collection of cleaning supplies *and* Angie. She could enjoy the next four months without any near-death experiences. Wasn't that what this was all about?

Laura pushed her luggage into the room, opened her suitcases and ran her hands over the clothing Willa had lent her for the semester. Laura still couldn't get over the way the expensive fabrics felt against her skin. The finely spun cashmeres, cottons and silks—even Willa's expensive jeans seemed to rest on her hips differently than her own from Old Navy.

I have to stop treating everything like it's new, Laura reminded herself as she started to unpack. *It's a dead giveaway that I don't belong here.*

Willa had given her a crash course in boarding school behavior, imparting a few nuggets of wisdom, such as: wealth is important but understated, sloppy is stylish but dirty is gross (hence Willa's overwhelming unpopularity) and it's okay to be smart but don't be a suck-up.

Unfortunately, that advice was barely enough to get Laura beyond the first week of school. Willa, by her own admission, wasn't exactly a boarding school success story. She had, in fact, semiseriously counseled Laura to "just do the opposite of anything I'd do and you'll be valedictorian by October."

Basically, Laura was on her own.

"Willa? Am I interrupting?"

Laura looked up and realized she'd left her door wide open. A young woman stood in the doorway.

"Uh, no," Laura said, trying to muster her best "I'm-nice-but-please-don't-bug-me" smile.

"Great." The woman moved breezily into the room and plopped onto the desk, which creaked in protest.

Laura bent over her suitcase, pretending to fold a shirt but instead studying the woman. She was tiny—and her short, straight brown hair was streaked with gray. She wore a white tank top under overalls, and her bare feet were tan. A small ruby stud winked at Laura from her left nostril.

"So, how do you like Fenwick so far?"

Laura shrugged. "It looks great. I mean, I just got here a few minutes ago."

The woman fingered a silver chain around her neck. "Well, I just wanted to come down and introduce myself. I'm your dorm advisor, Jenna Palmer. You're supposed to call me Ms. Palmer but

I hate that, so around the dorm you can call me Jenna. I teach dance at Fenwick—I've been here for about ten years—and I'm actually an alum myself. Class of ninety-three. So if you have any questions, please feel free to knock. I'm upstairs in two thirty-four."

"Thanks. I will," Laura said, relieved she wasn't living on the same floor as this woman. It could pose a threat to her anonymity. Plus, she hated when adults told you to call them by their first name. It was impossible to remember and they always got annoyed when you forgot, because then they felt old.

"Great. Listen, I gotta go. I'm making my 'welcome' rounds today." Jenna hopped off the desk and stretched, then slid across the room, her tiny dancer's feet barely making a sound on the cheap carpet. "Nice meeting you, Willa."

"Thanks. You too."

Laura shut the door and leaned against it, lost in thought. Ms. Palmer had thought she was Willa, so she'd obviously pulled this off. One person down, an entire campus to go.

Someone was knocking on the door.

Laura's pulse rose, her breath coming in uneven spurts through her mouth and nose. It was Ms. Palmer. Definitely. She'd come back with the authorities. Campus police. Or worse—the Pogues. Laura had lasted ten minutes at Fenwick.

Laura opened the door, steeling herself for the very worst.

She blinked. She blinked again. Then she realized that she was still holding her breath and was beginning to feel a little light-headed, so she focused on breathing. She still felt dizzy but that had less to do with oxygen and more to do with the boy who was standing in the hallway.

He somehow managed to be tall and thin but athletic-looking at the same time. Laura's eyes traveled across the planes of his face, over the strong jaw and high cheekbones, absorbing his deep blue eyes and the short, light brown hair.

It was, she realized, too good to be true. Guys who looked like this never knocked on her door. They asked her for help in chemistry but then didn't bother to apologize when they jostled her in the hallway. They saw her without ever really seeing her.

But to repeat: this guy *had* knocked on her door. This boy was standing in front of her. Right now.

"Uh, hi," he said, his eyebrows wrinkling slightly. He looked mildly surprised. "Willa?"

Once again, Laura waited for the apple effect to overwhelm her cheeks. The real Laura Melon couldn't talk to guys—especially cute ones—and when she absolutely had to she said something embarrassing and then tortured herself about it for months.

But she wasn't Laura anymore. And somehow, her body could tell. "I am," she said smoothly. *There is no doubt in my mind that I am who I say I am; that I should be here, talking to you.*

"Oh, great." He looked relieved. "I'm Caleb—Caleb Blake. You, uh, don't know me or anything but our parents are friends and my mom asked me to introduce myself. She was kind of dead set on it, actually. I tried to call over the summer—did you get any of my messages?"

"I'm sorry," she said, shaking her head. "I had kind of an intense summer, getting ready for school and everything. I know it was rude—I'm sorry."

Caleb laughed. "Don't worry about it. I'm the one who should be apologizing, really. I felt bad calling so much, but my mother kept making me. She gets something into her head and she kind of can't let it go. . . . Anyway, mind if I check out your room? I'm a little jealous you're in Hub. I was going to live here last year, but then did a study abroad in Italy and had to give up the room."

"Wow, Italy." Laura stepped aside, wondering if they were breaking some sort of coed visitation rule. Willa hadn't mentioned anything about it since Laura wasn't supposed to be receiving guests—male or female. And Laura couldn't ask since she was supposed to be a seasoned boarding school student.

"Yeah. Fenwick has a program in Florence. A lot of the students go. It was pretty amazing," Caleb said, glancing around the room. He whistled. "Whoa, this is sweet. You really lucked out."

Laura stared at him. He was joking, right? Where was his dorm room? Guantánamo Bay? She waited for his laughter, but there was none. He was serious.

"It's great," Laura agreed, trying to keep a straight face. "I know."

Caleb leaned against the wall and grinned. Laura smiled back, appreciating the way his eyes caught the light.

Would it be rude to ask him to stand there for the next four months? she wondered.

"So," he said, "will you please do me a favor and ask me a few questions about Fenwick? That way maybe my mom will finally leave me alone."

Laura laughed. "Actually," she said, grabbing her course guide out of her bag, "I do have some questions."

Caleb glanced down at the book, which was paper-clipped, bookmarked and covered with Post-it notes.

He grinned. "I'd better have a seat."

"Oh, please," Laura said. She pulled out the desk chair and watched as he settled in. "But actually—well—I guess I should've asked this from the very start, but, do you like Fenwick? I've been reading a lot about the school over the summer, but I was wondering . . ."

"You were wondering if you'll want to hang yourself from a gargoyle by Thanksgiving break?"

Actually, she was more interested in knowing if every boarding school kid shared Willa's attitude toward academia, but she'd start wherever Caleb wanted to.

"It's pretty cool here," he said. "I mean, for a school. They do kill you junior year—I'm just warning you. It's rough. Even in Italy, it was bad. But I have to say, I never thought about transferring." He laughed. "Don't tell anyone but I might even miss this place next year."

"You're graduating?" Laura asked. She found herself wondering where he was applying to college and what he wanted to major in, but then remembered that she wasn't supposed to be getting to know Caleb.

The thought suddenly struck Laura as tragic.

"Uh-huh," Caleb said. He reached for her course book. "Okay, what did you want to know?"

Twenty minutes later, they wove their way through the quad, toward the dining hall. "Thanks so much for all your help," Laura said. She meant it, too. Caleb had given her the lowdown on all the teachers—which one's courses to take and which ones to steer clear of—and now her schedule was pretty much complete.

"No problem," he said, giving a good-natured shrug. He stopped suddenly and turned to look at her. "You know, you're a lot different than I expected. I mean, my parents told me a little about you, but you're so completely—I don't know. You're into your classes and interested in school." He shrugged again. "I guess I'm just surprised."

Laura swallowed. She'd done it again. She couldn't completely stifle herself—it was impossible. She didn't want to, either.

Okay. You pulled this one off the last time. You can do it again. He believes you. Just stay with it. If you believe, he will too. You can go anywhere as someone else.

"You know, I did a lot of thinking this summer," she said. "Remember, that's why I didn't have time to call you back?"

Caleb laughed. "Well, then—"

"Hey, handsome!"

A small auburn-haired girl suddenly fell into step beside them and grabbed Caleb's hand. Upon later reflection, Laura would redefine the move as a hand-snatch.

"Oh, hey, Courtney." Either Caleb had decided to ignore the lilliputian's rudeness or he was simply too mellow a guy for that sort of thing to even register.

Laura's heart was sinking slowly in her chest. *Please don't say it,* she thought desperately. *I'll know, okay? But you don't have to say the words out loud.*

"Laura, I'd like you to meet my girlfriend, Courtney Wilton."

18

Elite women typically do not describe themselves as privileged or see their early childhood socialization as having been vastly different from that of girls in other social classes.
—*The Power of Good Deeds: Privileged Women and the Social Reproduction of the Upper Class*
Diana Kendall

Willa drifted through Laura's apartment, noting the comfortably worn furniture, the stucco walls and the soft, frayed area rugs. She had to memorize the whole thing—rooms, knick-knacks and cabinets—by the time Angie arrived, or else her cover would be totally blown.

Kicking off her shoes, Willa flopped onto the living room couch and sank into the softly worn cushions. She leaned her head back slightly and from this position was able to study the entire room.

The mismatched furniture and cheerful walls were so cozy, so inviting. And everywhere you looked there were pictures of

Laura and her mother from various stages of their life together. In every single one, they were laughing or hugging.

Willa stared down at her hands. The only photographs her parents hung in their houses were of her mother, back in her debutante days. The few baby pictures they had of Willa had been professionally taken and they all looked the same: she wore stiff, overly starched dresses and looked completely miserable.

Enough. She wasn't a Pogue—not for the next few months, anyway. *This* was her living room now. These were her photos— her happy memories.

They were on loan. That was the deal.

Willa strode down the hall toward her bedroom, mentally recording the number of doorways, light fixtures and closets along the way. She stepped inside and looked around.

Her mouth fell open as her toes curled in delight. "Adorable," she said. It was tiny, sure, but it was cozy. A bookshelf was built into one wall and the floor was covered with a pretty aquamarine and coral area rug. The walls were painted sky-blue and the quilt on Laura's daybed picked up all the colors.

The room was so great. It was *so* Laura.

But what was that smell?

Wincing, she sniffed at the air again. Was that *garbage?* It couldn't be—Laura was such a neat freak. Willa looked around the room for the source of the smell.

"Ahhh," she said as her eyes landed on the rolled-up zebra skin rug, which lay slumped in one corner of the room. So *this* was Angie's attempt at interior design.

Willa approached the rug and nudged it with her toe. It

unrolled about a foot. She pinched her nose shut and leaned down for a closer look.

It stank, sure. And the stains looked pretty bad. But Willa could kind of see where Angie was coming from. The rug—at one point—had probably been really expensive. Willa was pretty sure her parents had something like it in their New York town house.

Wait. Hadn't Laura passed along some sort of cleaning recommendation for carpet stains and odors?

Still holding her nose, Willa scooped up the malodorous rug and carried it toward the kitchen, where she spread it out on the linoleum floor. As she unfolded the last corner, a CD skidded across the room. Willa walked over and picked it up.

"The Professor's Got Yellow Fever." She laughed.

Some background music would be nice while she cleaned. Besides, Angie was definitely going to mention this mix, so Willa figured she ought to listen.

She walked over to the counter and popped the CD into a Discman that was hooked up to some tiny speakers.

Everything in this place is so cute, she thought.

Static crackled through the room. "Mellow Yellow" burst through the speakers.

"This had better work," Willa muttered as she assembled the supplies and dipped a scrub brush into a bucket filled with warm water, ammonia, white vinegar and laundry detergent. She'd initially forgotten the rubber gloves and her skin was red and throbbing from the ammonia.

Her hands moved over the rug in smooth, gentle strokes. The song was vaguely familiar. Then Willa's hand froze. *What the—?*

A new voice had joined the mix. It was large and booming, yet undeniably female.

Angie was now with the band.

It was no Lubé Special, but the mix was fun in a goofy sort of way. Willa went back to work. She worked through Angie's karaoke versions of "Yellow Submarine" and "Big Yellow Taxi." She even found herself humming along.

Somewhere near the end of "Tie a Yellow Ribbon Round the Old Oak Tree," the white stripes on the zebra skin rug had become purer than a debutante cotillion.

Willa stripped off her rubber gloves, her nostrils flaring slightly as she sucked down the new scent of clean. Staring down at the slick fur, her eyes traced the bold black and white stripes, mesmerized by the sharp contrast.

I did that, she thought as her chest rose with pride. Her first cleaning job had been a success. It felt strange. Strange but good.

"I just need to keep this up," she said, running her fingers over the rug's smooth, sponged surface. "I hope Angie likes it."

Every single roommate Willa had ever had—and there had been many—hated her. It didn't matter who they were—artists, jocks, satan worshippers, prom queens—the one thing they all shared was an instantaneous dislike of Willa. In her most paranoid moments, she even suspected they'd formed some sort of anti-Willa secret society, complete with a special handshake and logo—her head with a slash through it or something.

"Maybe this was a really bad idea," Willa muttered. The ammonia burned her eyes; anxiety had her heart thumping. "It was *my* bad idea. Laura's not despised everywhere she goes. I am. That'll probably tip Angie off just a *little*."

She reached into her back pocket and grabbed her phone.

```
boardgirl: having panic attack. help!
lubespecial: when i'm stressed i play
guitar.
boardgirl: but i don't play guitar.
lubespecial: is that why ur stressed?
```

Willa snapped her phone shut. Her stomach issued a long, low wail.

She walked over to the counter and grabbed a can of Pringles. She had to call Fenwick immediately and tell Laura to get out of there. It was that simple. This was an emergency. They could switch back tonight and maybe nobody would notice.

With a shaking hand, Willa flipped her cell open again. Suddenly a human tidal wave crashed through the apartment. Willa, her Pringles and a chair were lifted off the linoleum floor in one movement. The phone shot out of her hand and spiraled through the air like a model airplane.

"Hi, Angie," she croaked, struggling for breath.

Angie tossed her to the floor in what had to be a WWE regulation body drop. Standing beside Angie was a pale, thin boy. Willa remembered Laura's mentioning something about Angie having a boyfriend.

"Hi, Laura," he said, extending his hand. His voice was mild and Willa couldn't help noticing how tiny his hand was compared to Angie's. "It's so nice to finally meet you." He glanced admiringly in Angie's direction. "Angie's so excited about living with you."

Willa tried to sound relaxed. "Thanks. It's gonna be great."

"Great?" Angie boomed. "Professor! This is amazing!" She turned to Glenn. "Sorry about that. I'm so bad with introductions. I always forget."

Glenn laughed. "It's okay. I managed."

Angie pumped her head up and down as she turned to Willa. "I can't believe how long it's been, right? Me and all my emergencies. I'm just about ready to throw my beeper off a high dive!" She laughed good-naturedly. "But I'm so psyched about moving in. I mean, I'll miss our parents and everything, but it's just so cool we've got the place to ourselves. . . . *Wait a minute!*"

Willa's cheeks flamed as the floor slipped slowly out from underneath her feet. She dug her toes into her shoes and tried to steady herself but couldn't seem to find the proper balance.

I knew this wasn't going to work, she thought miserably. She waited for the blow that would bring pain and darkness.

Suddenly, a huge smile spread over Angie's thick features. "You look great, Professor!" she shrieked.

Willa's jaw fell slack. "*What?*"

"Oh, don't get me wrong," Angie thundered on. "You were pretty that first time I met you. But just a little scrawny, you know? But now, step *back!* You're beautiful!" She turned to Glenn. "Now don't you get any funny ideas, okay?"

Glenn held up his hands. "Promise."

Willa was still reeling from the surprise compliment when Angie caught sight of the zebra skin rug. Her face lit up.

"Did you do that, Professor?" she asked, not waiting for a response. " 'Cause it looks great! I shoulda known you'd know what to do with it. Do you care where we put it, 'cause . . ."

But Willa was totally zoned out. She couldn't remember the last time anyone had complimented her looks. Willa had, in the past, received plenty of negative feedback, of course. Over the years her mother had called her chunky and tubby and—when she cared to be tactful—big. But nobody, not her mother or father or anyone else, had ever told her she was beautiful. They hadn't even said she was average.

Willa watched as her new roommate leaned over the rug and ran her hands along the pelt.

This is going to be okay, she thought.

19

Great new look! Great new formula!!
—Zout Stain Remover

It's really a good thing that Caleb has a girlfriend, Laura told herself for the millionth time.

She stared down at the brown plasticine substance on her plate—Salisbury steak, according to the Fenwick dining hall—and frowned.

No wonder Willa was so obsessed with food, if she'd been subjected to this stuff every night.

Laura's eyes traveled across the room to Caleb and Courtney's oh-so-cozy table in a quiet corner of the cafeteria. Caleb had invited her to join them, but Laura had declined, insisting that she had some last-minute summer reading to finish. Everyone had known it was a lie, but he hadn't pushed. The murderous look on Courtney's face, combined with her death-lock grip, had probably weighed heavily in his decision.

So now Laura was alone. None of the happy, chattering voices bouncing around the dining hall were meant for her.

The current of mingled conversations pulled her away from her tray and Laura found her gaze drifting back to Caleb. He was talking, his face animated and expressive, his hair tousled.

Laura ducked her head. Why was she torturing herself?

This is the way it was supposed to be, she thought, staring at the empty seat next to her. *I'm not here to become homecoming queen.*

And Caleb Blake wasn't part of the plan either.

Laura stood and lifted her tray, her back straight and stiff. *Just pull the Band-Aid off quickly,* she thought.

As she walked toward the dorm, she forced herself to digest every magnificent building, walkway and blade of grass that comprised the quad.

When I'm by myself I don't have any distractions, she thought as she leaned over to read a plaque outside the infirmary. *I can really get to know the campus history.*

"Willa Pogue?"

She started. A middle-aged woman in a blue terry-cloth jogging suit was standing next to her, perhaps a bit too close, scrutinizing her through intense brown eyes.

"I'm sorry," the woman said. "I didn't mean to scare you."

"That's okay."

How does this woman know Willa? Laura wondered. Tiny dots of perspiration decorated her forehead.

"I'm Mrs. Flemming," the woman said, extending her hand.

"Willa Pogue."

"I thought so. I manage the infirmary and since everyone usually comes to see me at some point during the year I try to introduce myself—even before you really need me," Mrs. Flemming explained. She was practically glowing at the thought of Laura's future illness.

"Uh, that's nice." Laura felt like her head was about to explode. Mrs. Flemming knew Willa?

Laura excused herself as quickly as possible. She was annoyed at Willa for not doing her research. This was so typical. All Willa had to do was look at the faculty listings and Laura could've been better prepared.

There were two girls sitting on the porch of Hubbard House drinking bottled water. One had curly black hair that she wore tied back in a ponytail. The other had straight, light brown hair. Their tennis racquets were in cases, leaning off to the side.

Laura climbed the steps, unsure of what do with her eyes. Should she look down at her feet or should she try to say hello, maybe introduce herself, instead? She wasn't supposed to make friends, but she didn't want people to think she was rude, either.

She was still mid-debate when ponytail girl waved. "Hey," she said, looking up. "Are you Willa?"

Oh no, thought Laura. *Not again.*

"Uh, yeah." She forced her voice to sound normal. "I am."

"Hi. I'm Alice."

The girl sitting next to her smiled. "I'm Brewer. Nice to meet you."

"Thanks. You too."

Alice reached back and ran a hand through her ponytail. "So, are you unpacked and everything?"

"More or less. Are you?"

"So-so. Have you met Jenna?"

Laura nodded. "She seemed sort of interesting."

The girls laughed.

"That's one way to phrase it," said Brewer. "Listen, whatever you do, don't take her whole 'I'm totally relaxed' vibe seriously. It's all an act."

"It is?" Laura pictured Jenna in her head, with her overalls and bare feet.

"She's super-uptight. She sees anything against the rules, she'll tell," Alice said. "Last year, she got eleven kids expelled for drinking on a school trip to see the Ballet Folklórico in Mexico City."

Laura had already been planning to stay away from Jenna, so this wouldn't change anything. "Thanks for the warning."

"No problem."

"We're on three if you need anything," Alice said. She took another swig of water. "Do you play?"

"What?"

Alice gestured toward the tennis racquets. "I was just wondering if you played," she repeated.

"Alice and I play for Fenwick and we're always trying to recruit people," Brewer explained.

"Sorry," Laura said, shaking her head. It was the most honest she'd been all day.

"Too bad. You look like you're in great shape," Brewer said absently, peeling a strip of paint off the porch floor.

Laura waved good-bye and headed back to her room. Everyone on campus seemed to know Willa already. How, though?

Laura unlocked her door and sat down at Willa's Mac. Was this an emergency? It definitely felt like one.

```
willypoo2: help! freaking out. every-
one knows u! this is bad bad bad.
boardgirl: u r freaking out cuz u r a
freak. Nobody nose me.
```

```
willypoo2: they do.
boardgirl: consult websters for
definition of emergency. got 2 go.
Angie and i r making fluffernutters.
```

Well, that was helpful. And what was a Fluffernutter?

Laura clicked off her computer and turned around. For the first time, she spotted a package on her bed, with a note attached. She hadn't noticed it before, in her panicked state. She leaned down to read the curling, flowery cursive:

Willa—This arrived for you in today's mail but I forgot to give it to you during our meet and greet. Sorry! Hope you don't mind that I let myself in. Peace, J. P.

Jenna Palmer had a key to this room.

From head to toe, every part of Laura's body snapped to attention as she scanned the room looking for clues—anything that might betray her. She knew she should be outraged by the obvious invasion of privacy but, oddly, she felt nothing. Her primary concern—actually her only concern—was jeopardizing the plan.

Laura's eyes traveled over Willa's shiny metallic laptop, the Pogues' leather trunks, the expensive borrowed clothing. The shabby room looked ridiculous packed with all the overpriced luxury items.

It was, Laura realized with some surprise, your stereotypical boarding school room. She was willing to bet that her room looked like every other dorm room on campus.

I'm safe, Laura thought. *For now.*

The package was from Mrs. Pogue. Or rather, it had been sent by Emory as dictated by Mrs. Pogue. Laura recognized the firm, straight printing at once:

> Willa—the following materials were sent to the Newport house accidentally. Please be sure to correct the error with the registrar. Additionally, enclosed are some items for your room.
> Enjoy, Mother

Laura slid a thin book out of the box and turned it over. It was the Fenwick student directory.

"It's not against the rules to find out Caleb's campus address," she reasoned as she attacked the book, her fingers flipping to the Bs.

"Wait a minute." Laura was so surprised that she sat down on the stained mattress she'd sworn she wouldn't touch until she'd scoured it with disinfectant.

There were pictures. The student directory had *pictures*. They were there, right beside each student's name and home and school address.

Laura turned to the Ps and gasped. Willa stared up at her, a defiant glint in her eye. There was a star by her name, indicating that she was a new student.

The picture had been taken in front of Pogue Hall. Mrs. Pogue must have sent it when she mailed the deposit.

Like a key sliding into a lock, Laura's whole day suddenly clicked into place.

She paced the short expanse of her room. Right now, every student at Fenwick was probably cracking open their directory, if they hadn't already. Was this cause for worry?

No. The people around campus didn't know Willa—they had no inside information. They'd just seen one picture of her, which was fine since she and Willa looked *exactly* alike.

She reached over and jostled the care package. Two hot pink throw pillows flopped onto the floor. One read: GET FIT, NOT FAT! and the second, a stuffed scale with an anxious look on its face, pleaded: PLEASE GO LIGHT ON ME.

How could anyone survive with a mother like that?

Laura felt a tiny corner of her heart break off and fly away.

Slowly, she packed up the pillows—and Mrs. Pogue's note—and dumped them all into the garbage.

20

A young lady, on leaving school, is expected
to take a more important place in her
father's house; she must go into society; she
must perform her part for the poor, the sick
and the afflicted; she must assist her
mother in domestic affairs.
—*The Young Lady's Friend*
John Farrar

At 7 AM Angie was already in the kitchen standing over the
stove. The entire apartment smelled like IHOP.

"What are you doing?" Willa said, stumbling in and rubbing
her eyes.

"Hey, Professor! C'mon in!" Angie boomed, waving her
spatula by way of invitation. "I'm just finishing up."

Willa sat down at the table as Angie joined her, bringing
a mountain of blueberry pancakes. The table was also loaded
with scrambled eggs, bacon, sausage and a huge pitcher of hot
chocolate.

Willa watched as Angie helped herself to a fat stack. No
guilt, apology or stress. Last night, Angie had fixed herself a

giant salad, not because she was dieting but because she'd been hungry and in the mood for a salad. Her motives hadn't run any deeper. Angie's meals were free; they didn't come wrapped in emotion.

Willa had never had a free snack in her entire life.

Willa served herself, completely disregarding any attempt at portion control. It was the first time, she realized, she'd ever been able to eat with someone else and not feel shame or embarrassment. At home, the dining room was a war zone, her mother's eagle eye a tracking missile. Within seconds, Sibby could slice portions in half and blast dangerous carbohydrates to smithereens.

The constant mealtime battles had pushed Willa into a permanent state of food paranoia. It followed her everywhere, to every table and every other location. And no matter what she did, she could feel herself being judged in terms of what she ate.

Until this morning.

Angie reached for the syrup. "Uh, do you always cook such big breakfasts?"

"Yeah, usually," Angie said. "I try, unless I get a real emergency—you know, like a busted impeller or something. It's the most important meal of the day." She pounded the back of Willa's chair and the entire room seemed to shake. "Gotta keep your energy up, right?"

Willa frowned slightly as Angie's comment sank in. It was true. She did need to keep her energy up. She had a job now.

And last night she'd dreamt she'd gotten fired.

An arrow of pain shot through her temples as she pulled a crumpled schedule out of her pocket. Willa liked to keep it with her, even though she'd memorized it ages ago:

Monday	Tuesday	Wednesday	Thursday	Friday
Mortimer	Pogue Hall	Mortimer	Pogue Hall	Young
(AM)	(AM)	(AM)	(AM)	(AM)
Watson		Watson		
(PM)		(PM)		

She cleaned Pogue Hall—her house—today.

"Listen, I'd better get going," she said, swallowing a last bite of pancake and scraping back her chair. "I have to clean Pogue Hall today. I, uh, should probably get an early start. The kid just left for school so her room is probably a real mess."

"Oh, okay." Angie stood and walked over to the refrigerator. She pulled out a large shopping bag and passed it to Willa. "Here, I made you lunch when I was making mine. Just a couple of drinks and sandwiches and some of those fruit snack things. Oh, and I stuck in some granola. You know, in case you get hungry between jobs."

"Thanks, Angie." The lunch felt as if it weighed nearly ten pounds. Still, Willa was really touched. She wondered if Laura had any idea how sweet her stepsister-to-be was. "That was really nice."

"Nah, forget it. Listen, Glenn's coming over tonight. We'll all hang out." Angie dove back into her breakfast as Willa grabbed her keys. "Happy dusting!"

Willa let herself into her own house through the servants' entrance and changed into the uniform she'd borrowed from Laura's mother. It itched around her neck.

She eased the cleaning caddy through halls she'd known forever. Concerned that someone would recognize her, she kept her eyes glued to the floor until, after about ten minutes, she realized there was no need for caution. She and Laura had purposely arranged the schedule to coincide with Pogue Hall's emptiest time of day. Plus, the regular staff—anyone who would recognize her—traveled with her parents. The house was pretty much deserted.

As she shoved the caddy toward her bedroom door, a memory rose to the front of her brain: She was seven years old and had somehow become convinced that inanimate objects had feelings. A rarely used vase could feel lonely, a broken end table depressed.

All of a sudden, Pogue Hall had been jam-packed with suicidal appliances and it had become Willa's mission to save each and every one. She'd run from room to room, flicking lights on and off, crooning words of comfort to various pieces of furniture. The phase had come to a catastrophic halt after Willa tried to comfort her mother's Ming vase. She'd tried to explain that she'd been practicing a unique form of CPR, but her mother had been in no mood to listen.

Surprise, surprise.

Her bedroom now was exactly as she'd left it: the bed was unmade, a few items of clothing lay scattered on the floor and the curtains were drawn.

Not bad, Willa thought as she pushed the cleaning caddy into the room. *I should be out of here in no time at all.*

It took her almost twenty minutes just to clean the floor. She had no idea where all the dust had come from. And vacuuming an area rug? Forget it.

Finally—*finally*—she moved to the curtains.

"I don't even want to know *what* this is," she muttered, scrubbing a Clorox-and-salt solution over an angry black splotch.

After almost three straight hours of cleaning, Willa was done with her bedroom. It looked great but she was a mess, with blisters on every finger and carpet burn on her knees.

"These uniforms are the stupidest things ever invented," she muttered, scratching at her neck with one hand, rubbing her shoulder with the other. "It'd be so much easier to clean in sweats."

Her eyes drifted over to her freshly made bed. She'd give anything for a catnap—she'd forfeit an entire day's pay if she could just curl up for ten minutes . . . or maybe an hour—

This isn't your paycheck to forfeit, she reminded herself. *And that's not your bed.*

She'd seriously underestimated the amount of work this entailed. She'd thought she could slip on her iPod and listen to Lubé Special all day. But she needed to focus while she worked. Music was a distraction. Cleaning an entire house was way harder than cleaning one smelly rug. And her schedule was packed with houses.

Inhaling deeply, Willa let her eyes wander around her room— her clean, sweet-smelling room. She'd spent thousands of hours in here over the years but had never—not once—contributed to its upkeep. No, she'd had to become someone else to do that.

Still, her finished product was impressive.

I did this, she thought. *And I know it was me.*

Maybe it didn't qualify her as the next Meryl Streep, but it felt amazing all the same.

She made a mental note to apologize to Laura. This was one tough job.

Willa pushed the cleaning caddy down the hall. It had been years since she'd been in her parents' room and now, stepping inside, she felt a chill run down her spine. The room was decorated in white and ice-blue—ice-blue couches and curtains, white duvet and floors, thick white and blue striped wallpaper. The only real signs of life were her mother's prized debutante clippings. Otherwise, the place was completely sterile—like it had been hermetically sealed or something.

At least this won't take long, Willa thought as she rolled the cleaning caddy into the middle of the room. She grabbed the Swiffer and gently brushed the pictures (*Laura was right, how could anyone dust without a Swiffer? It picked up everything*) as her eyes skimmed the clippings.

There she was: "Newport Beauty Sibby Welles." In this particular photo, taken at something called the Cinderella Ball, the caption described her mother as "fresh and glowing."

Willa moved onto another clipping—a write-up of Newport's Medallion Ball. This article called her mother both "eye-catching" and "stunning."

Willa had passed these pictures a million times—she'd grown up with them. But she'd never really *looked* at them before. They were always such a thorn in her side—just one more reminder of how she'd failed to follow in her parents' footsteps.

She wasn't Pogue material. And she wasn't deb material, either.

Her eyes slid over a picture of her mother, smiling and pretty, at the Gold and Silver Ball. At this event, her mother was supposedly "breathtaking."

Willa walked up and down the display of articles, comparing

adjectives. They were all variations on a theme: "radiant," "sparkling," "charming" . . .

Sadly, these were not words Willa would ever use to describe her mother. If pressed, Willa wasn't even sure she'd be able to describe her mother at all. Other than Sibby Pogue's fanatic worship of tennis and golf—and, of course, her "dazzling" deb past—Willa didn't really know her mother.

She didn't really know either of her parents. Their presence was shadowy at best, their most memorable quality being the intense disapproval they expressed toward her and everything she did. It coated them like barbed wire, preventing any softer, more positive sentiments from slipping out—or in.

It was really sort of sad.

Willa glanced down at her watch and gasped. She'd wasted almost thirty minutes on these lame pictures. She still had to clean the other six bedrooms *and* be out of the house before the gardeners arrived in the late afternoon.

Besides, maybe she didn't know her mother because there simply wasn't much to know.

Need some adjectives to describe Sibby Pogue? she thought. *How about "vain"? "Vain," "shallow" and "preppy." Those are perfect.*

Willa turned her back on her mother's glory days and shoved the cleaning caddy out of the room, slamming the door behind her.

She didn't look back until she was in another wing of the house.

21

Trust the Original
—Pine-Sol

Every once in a while, Laura's mother won the Lotto. It was never big money—a few hundred dollars at most—but it was still pretty thrilling. She celebrated by purchasing name-brand groceries rather than the usual generic items. The next morning, she and Laura would sit in the kitchen and savor the taste of Tropicana fresh-squeezed orange juice and Cheerios and Thomas' English muffins. The real thing always tasted better, no matter how hard the imitation tried.

Laura considered this rule as she walked across campus on her first day of classes.

It applied outside the grocery store, too.

Take Fenwick, for instance. Founded in the eighteenth century, the school was one of the oldest in the country. And after just one morning, Laura realized that her entire academic career had been a complete joke. Compared to Fenwick, her old high school reminded her of a brick sinking to the bottom of a pond.

This was the way school was supposed to be.

Laura glanced down at her schedule card. She had U.S.

history next. She hadn't seen Mr. Stade since the luncheon, but of all her classes, his was the one she was most excited about.

As she cut across the quad, Laura scanned the passing faces. It was a habit she'd developed—a bad habit—but she couldn't help it. She'd seen Caleb only once since that first day, tossing a Frisbee with a couple of guys.

Laura frowned as she yanked open the door to Regan Hall. This wasn't a constructive interest. First of all, it was against the rules—Willa would kill her. Second of all, he had a girlfriend.

And third—this thought was accompanied by a dull ache somewhere between her stomach and chest—he hadn't bothered to look her up again.

It was best to just forget about Caleb and all things social. Sometimes you had to just plow ahead and not dwell on things that were out of your control, like cute guys you couldn't have. She was happy with her schedule, right? She loved Fenwick— that was huge. How many kids actually liked school?

Finish your UConn application, enjoy this place . . . and move on, she thought as she reached the door.

The room was small, and the desks had been placed in a circle around the blackboard. As Laura slid into a chair near the window, she studied Mr. Stade's desk. It was covered with huge towers of paper as well as a few empty Styrofoam cups, but it showed no immediate signs of life. He clearly hadn't arrived yet.

Laura pictured Mr. Stade's house—history texts everywhere and a sink overflowing with dirty dishes. The image didn't gross her out at all. It appealed to her, actually. He was probably the quintessential absentminded professor.

"Hey, Willa, mind if I sit here?"

That *voice*. Laura had been looking for him all over campus, but he'd managed to slip into class without her even noticing. She'd been too busy thinking about Mr. Stade's dirty dishes.

Stay calm, she thought, her heart pounding.

"Sure," she said, just as her hand slammed the tip of her notepad, sending it flying straight into Caleb's face. It swatted him on the nose before flopping to the ground. A few stray papers drifted to the floor in its wake, like confetti thrown at a parade float.

"Oh my god, are you okay?" Laura said. She had a flashback to her old self. This was definitely something the real Laura Melon would've done around a cute guy. Maybe she was back.

It wasn't a cheerful thought.

"Whoa. I can sit somewhere else if you want." Caleb laughed as he leaned forward to pick up the notepad. "Honesty is always the best policy, Willa."

"You're taking this class?" she asked, hoping her cheeks weren't too red. "I mean, aren't you a senior?"

Caleb pulled a laptop out of his bag. "Yeah, but I was in Italy for a semester junior year, remember? I never got to take Stade's class."

Why hadn't he mentioned that, back on that first day? He hadn't said anything about it, which was weird. Could he have switched his schedule around—maybe taken the class because he knew she was enrolled too?

Don't flatter yourself, she thought as Mr. Stade walked into the room. *He sat next to you, that's all. He's just being nice.*

"Good morning," Mr. Stade said, smiling. "Welcome back."

His eyes found Willa's and his smile grew wider. "And for those of you new to Fenwick, welcome for the first time. This class is United States history, 1898 to 1945. If you're supposed to be someplace else—say PE or studio art—now is the time to go find that place."

He paused politely as a tall, red-faced kid muttered an apology about an SAT tutorial and stumbled out the door.

Caleb rolled his eyes. There were a few snickers.

"Now then," continued Mr. Stade as he passed out the syllabus, "I am assuming all cell phones are off and all laptops are either plugged in or are running on full batteries."

A few students leaned over and turned off their cells.

"Why are we in a circle?" said a tall brunette near the door.

"Ah, thank you for not raising your hand, Cricket," replied Mr. Stade as everyone laughed, including the tall brunette. "I arranged the seats in a circle because this class is not your typical history class. It's not a lecture. It's more of a seminar. I encourage discussion and analysis—and debates, of course."

Laura stared down at her syllabus. She wasn't used to talking in class—class discussions were unheard of at her old high school. She couldn't really see herself debating anyone.

"If you check your syllabus," Mr. Stade continued, "you'll also note that in addition to chapter exams you're responsible for two papers. You may hand in these papers at any time, on any topic of your choice, so long as both the topic and outline are preapproved by yours truly." He looked around. "Are there any questions?"

There were some scattered nos, a bunch of head shakes and a few yawns.

"Great. Shall we get started?" Mr. Stade pushed off his desk and, with thick squeaky chalk, printed "1898" on the blackboard. "Okay, if you were living in the U.S. during this period, what was on your mind—other than the millennium countdown and early preparations for what I'm sure were a slew of absolutely fantastic New Year's parties?" Mr. Stade turned back to face the class.

Patches of laughter and a few hoots broke out around the room. Laura jotted the words "Spanish-American War" in her notebook but kept her arm firmly planted by her side.

"That'd be McKinley's Spanish-American War," Caleb said, his own hand semiraised as he answered the question.

"Good. What else can you tell us about it? Anyone?"

Again there was a silence and again Caleb jumped in, rattling off facts and dates. A few other students commented here and there while Mr. Stade shaped the discussion, but, for the most part, Caleb had the floor.

Head lowered over her notebook, Laura took copious notes and tried to conceal her astonishment. She'd never—not for a second—assumed Caleb was an idiot.

But nothing had prepared her for *this*. It was shocking. Caleb *was* the History Channel.

Laura sat up a little straighter in her chair and squared her shoulders.

But so was she.

Any hesitation she might have felt about speaking in class suddenly evaporated. The new Laura Melon thrived on healthy competition.

"A lot of people compare the Spanish-American War to the war in Iraq," Caleb was saying.

"Why do you think that is?" probed Mr. Stade.

"Well, it was the first U. S. intervention on foreign soil."

Laura's hand felt like it was buzzing. Slowly, deliberately, she raised it into the air.

"Yes, Willa?"

"But you're not including attacks on the nations of the Apaches, the Seminole, the Cherokee—and a ton of others I'm forgetting." She turned to Caleb. "No offense."

"What's she talking about?" a guy in a baseball cap asked.

"She's talking about the Native American population," Mr. Stade said, smiling. "So, Willa, why do you think people compare the wars? Or don't you agree?"

"Oh, no, I see a comparison," Laura said as she turned to Caleb apologetically. "Only, uh, sorry, but I do think it's more complicated than just the occupation."

Caleb spread out his palm. "No—please. Go for it."

"Well, both invasions involved freeing an oppressed group of people—in Cuba it was liberation from Spanish rule, while in Iraq it was Saddam Hussein, of course. . . ."

Laura continued talking, her voice clear and steady. A few of the other kids asked her questions, challenging her, but she never flinched. It was amazing how good this felt.

"Great work," Mr. Stade said as the bell rang, his eyes pausing momentarily on Laura before moving around the circle. "This bodes well for the rest of the semester. Keep it up. And keep those cell phones off, Brooks. I heard that, you know."

Everyone laughed and started to pack up their bags.

"You really know your stuff," Caleb said appreciatively, zipping his computer case. "How'd you get to be such a history geek?"

"How about you?" Laura teased, artfully dodging the question. "You're like a walking encyclopedia. Do you have a photographic memory or something?"

"I wish. No, my dad was a history major. You should see our Nantucket house. The library is packed with history books. It's a little weird."

They walked out of class together and Laura replayed his comment in her head. *Our Nantucket house. The library.* The words were like pins, popping her euphoria and reminding her of the different planets she and Caleb inhabited. He'd said it all so casually, like having a beautiful summer home was as normal as having an arm or a leg.

Did he know how lucky he was? Laura wondered. She watched him pass through the door, his computer case slung low on his shoulder. She hoped so. More than anything, she hoped so.

Some things about this reality would never seem normal to her. It wasn't hers, and no matter how hard she tried, there would always be something she just couldn't understand. She was the imitation, and the imitation always failed to measure up in some way or another. Always.

22

The tone of a household is determined by
the people who run it.
—*The Amy Vanderbilt Complete Book of Etiquette*

Cigarettes. Smokes. Butts. Fags.

Willa had found them by the boatload. Or, to be precise, she'd found a porcelain mallard stuffed to the beak with Lucky Strikes. Unfiltered.

"Yuck," she said. She twisted one of the thin sticks around in her fingers before letting it fall back inside the bird.

It had been an innocent enough discovery. She'd been dusting the Mortimers' living room when she noticed that the bird's head was loose and wobbling. Her attempt to fix it had resulted in an accidental decapitation.

As she glanced around the tartan living room, Willa's eyes sought out the Mortimer family picture. Hays and Muffin Mortimer and their three flaxen-haired children smiled at her from the top of a snowcapped mountain. All five wore the same Christmas sweater.

"*I don't smoke!*" the cherubic faces seemed to sing as Willa studied their blond innocence.

"Please," she admonished. "That duck didn't swim in here by himself."

A tall, thin woman rushed into the room. Her velvet headband looked like it had been surgically attached to her wheat-blond head.

Enter Muffin Mortimer.

Willa opened her mouth, then clamped it shut. She'd promised Laura to speak only when spoken to, right? Grabbing her Swiffer, she tried to look busy. She'd wait for Mrs. Mortimer to say hello first.

But the woman didn't seem to be in a talking mood. Breezing past Willa, she headed straight for the duck, snapped off its head and placed it noiselessly on the floor beside the mallard's glazed tail feathers. As one hand slid into the bird, her other hand worked its way through her light green Kelly bag and emerged with a sterling silver lighter. Smokes and fire in hand, Muffin glanced around the room, confirming that the coast was indeed clear. She allowed herself a small, congratulatory giggle before heading out onto the grand wooden deck for her afternoon smoke.

The mystery of the mallard was solved.

Unbelievable, Willa thought as the door slammed behind her employer. *It was like I wasn't even in the room. At all. It's almost like I was—*

"Invisible." Willa said the word out loud—and loudly—as if to prove just the opposite.

Laura had warned her about this, she realized as she trudged up the stairs toward the bedrooms.

Well, why didn't she elaborate? Willa wondered. *And she definitely knew about that duck. How annoying.*

Then Willa straightened, remembering Laura's words. *It's not something you can explain,* she'd said. She had a point. Besides, Willa had always been on the Mortimer side of the issue. How many times had she marched by a staff member—a cook or cleaning person—at Pogue Hall without saying hello? Laura and her mother were really the first employees she'd ever gotten to know. She'd always assumed that people disapproved of her, but maybe she was reading too much into things. Maybe they were simply waiting for her to be friendly. And since she never was, they weren't in return.

What a strange world she'd entered. All her life, Willa had been taught that success was standing out; her consistent failure to do so had repeatedly plagued her. But in her new role, blending in was more than acceptable—it was valued. And essential.

As early as this morning, Willa had seen nothing wrong with that philosophy. After all, this was what she'd always wanted: freedom from her family—from the Pogue name. And now, if these people couldn't see her, well, it was impossible to disappoint them, right?

But the scene in the living room had hardly been liberating. Mrs. Mortimer had treated her like less than nothing. The experience had been a lot more bruising than one of her parents' stupid lectures. She'd never really thought about it before, but now she knew: falling short of your potential was definitely not as bad as having no potential at all. And that was what these people thought of people like Laura and her mom.

Fresh guilt twisted Willa's stomach as she padded down the hallway.

Instinctively, she reached for her phone. A quick rally with Lubé would definitely bolster her spirits.

Willa froze midstep. What was she thinking? IM was off-limits during the day, no exceptions. Wow. One bad experience with a grown woman named Muffin and her carcinogenic duck, and she was quivering like Jell-O. *How insecure can I get?* she thought.

She was going to stick to the game plan. Regardless of the experience downstairs, this had to be better than Fenwick.

She really had to develop some thicker skin if she was going to do this job. Actually, forget the job. Thicker skin was a good idea in general. The world—especially hers—was filled with Muffins. And ducks. She just had to learn to ignore them.

"*Whatever,*" Willa muttered, grudgingly. "She still could've said hi. A little wave would've been nice."

The first door off the long, wide hallway wore a huge, hand-made DO NOT ENTER sign just above the knob. Written in bright pink and purple bubble letters, the words looked warm and inviting, so Willa hastily brushed it aside.

The room belonged to Phoebe Mortimer, the youngest member of the family and a sophomore at Greenwich Academy, the local prep school. Phoebe's bedroom was huge—almost as large as Willa's room at Pogue Hall—and made American Girl Place seem butch by comparison. Decorated entirely in hot pink and lavender, the place was coated in lace and ruffles (Laura was so right, ruffles were just the *worst* to clean—you had to shake and shake, and they never really did get completely clean, did they?). After only ten minutes, Willa sank down on the end of the bed for a little rest.

"Excuse me?"

It was hard to say what scared Willa more—the voice or that telltale smell of cigarette smoke. Willa jumped up and spun around. Mrs. Mortimer's head poked into the bedroom. She didn't look mad exactly, but she wasn't smiling, either.

"Um, I—I'm sorry," Willa stammered. What rotten timing! If she got Laura into trouble she'd kill herself. "I was cleaning and felt a little faint so I sat for, like, just a second, you know? Then I was—"

"I wanted to remind you that my daughter's scent is lavender."

"Her scent?"

"Lavender," Mrs. Mortimer repeated impatiently. "When you launder my daughter's sheets, please use the lavender water in the iron. My husband and I use the rosewater, while the boys get Crabtree and Evelyn's Spring Rain. I thought I should remind you, since it's been a few months."

"Uh, thanks," Willa said, but Mrs. Mortimer and her Lucky Strikes were already moving down the hall.

"Also, Phoebe's dirty field hockey uniforms are in her laundry basket," Mrs. Mortimer shouted over her shoulder. "It's the season now and she's the star center, so please don't let them sit."

"I won't," Willa replied, even though she knew nobody could hear her.

She walked over to the purple wicker hamper and flipped open the lid. It was stuffed with dirty clothes, but there was no field hockey uniform.

Great, she thought. She rolled up her sleeves and started looking.

Fifteen minutes later Willa was still looking. She'd collected the entire Mortimer family's dirty laundry, including their sheets and towels, but Phoebe's hockey uniform was still missing.

She was on the verge of giving up—she still had another house to clean—when she found a red gym bag with a hockey stick stitched on the front buried under a pile of stuffed animals in the closet. Inside were a pair of stiff new cleats, two round-trip ticket stubs to Grand Central Station and a pamphlet: "How to Care for Your New Tattoo."

"Looks like Muffin isn't the only Mortimer with a secret," Willa said, shaking the bag to see if she'd missed some hidden treasure. A paper flopped out onto the rug. It was riddled with angry-looking red slashes that Willa recognized immediately. A test. A *failed* test.

Phoebe Mortimer was failing geometry, according to her teacher. It said so at the top of the paper, along with a bright red "See me."

Willa felt a pang of sympathy. She'd taken geometry twice herself and had found the class impossible. It had somehow managed to get even more confusing the second time, with more shapes floating around in her brain.

On the back of the test, Phoebe had scribbled a note to someone:

Mom thinks I have practice every day after school so Seb and I are taking the train into the city. Cover for me if she stops by the field? ❤ *Phoebe*

Unbelievable, Willa thought. *Muffin's out on the porch chain-smoking while her daughter's in Manhattan with her boyfriend, getting tattooed like a member of Hells Angels.* What were the brothers doing? Boiling bodies down in the basement? Was the father polygamous?

Sufficiently creeped out, Willa finished up and beat a hasty retreat over to the Watsons'.

Unfortunately, the Watson residence was hardly an improvement. Willa had only just started cleaning the kitchen when a tiny woman laden with Bergdorf's bags exploded into the room.

"Come on," she snapped. "Quickly now."

Frozen with surprise, Willa stared at the woman. She was pretty but way too thin, and that thinness gave her face a hard, mean quality. And she was definitely wearing her weight in perfume. Willa could smell it from six feet away.

"Come on," the woman repeated.

Come on what? Willa thought.

"What's wrong with you? Are you waiting for a written invitation?" Mrs. Watson held out a garment bag, shaking it for emphasis.

"Oh," Willa said, relieved that she finally understood.

"Take everything upstairs to my dressing room and remove the clothing, then place the bags and boxes in the fireplace and burn them," instructed Mrs. Watson rapidly. "All receipts should go in the way, way back of my nightstand. Fast! My husband comes home early every Wednesday before golf. It is essential that he not see these items. Is that clear? Do you speak English?"

Her face on fire, heart pounding, Willa grabbed the shopping bags and ran.

At least Mrs. Watson had acknowledged her presence immediately, right?

As she dumped the clothes onto an overstuffed love seat in the master bedroom, Willa absorbed her surroundings. Never in her life—neither in Phoebe Mortimer's bedroom nor at Christmas—had she seen anything more overdecorated. Flowers in bright yellows, greens, purples and violets warred with shells, horses and three different kinds of plaid. Ornate balloon shades, blinds *and* curtains dressed each of the eight windows. The massive room was the emotionally disturbed offspring of Ralph Lauren and Laura Ashley.

The layout was confusing, too. Five different doors led from the room. Willa tried a few of them before she found Mrs. Watson's dressing room.

Willa's fingers moved quickly over tags and hangers, pulling and tearing until everything was hung up. She looked down at the mess of receipts in her hands and turned toward the two nightstands. She yanked one open.

It was filled with copies of *Playboy*.

Definitely Mr. Watson's side of the bed.

She walked over to the other side of the bed and shoved the receipts as far back into that nightstand's drawer as they would go.

I could switch the two hiding places, she thought, imagining the look on Mr. Watson's face when he reached for a *Playboy* and pulled out a fistful of clothing bills.

But then Mrs. Watson would fire her. Correction: Mrs.

Watson would fire Laura Melon. And Willa had promised Laura she'd behave herself.

Not that the Watsons don't deserve it, she thought, shaking her head. These families were awful.

Willa froze as she realized that her family was no better.

After all, didn't her parents think their daughter was safely ensconced up at Fenwick Academy?

"Just clean," she muttered as she gathered the shopping bags and boxes. "Just clean."

23

No messes too mean!
—Brillo

"Oh, honey, you should see me! I look like a beach bum! I've got the tan, the floppy hat, the flip-flops. You wouldn't recognize your own mother!"

As her mom's voice filtered through the phone in loud, staccato bursts, Laura leaned her head back and closed her eyes. "It sounds amazing. I'm so glad you're having a great time."

"I am, sweetie. I really am. And I'm just so proud of you, holding down the business like you are. You're the reason I was able to do this."

Laura swallowed. She'd dreaded this first conversation with her mother. Alone, walking around campus, Laura could push herself into the fantasy. Some days she almost believed her life here was real.

But the sound of her mother's voice ruined everything. It made pretending impossible. She'd known it would.

"It's nothing," she whispered.

"It's not nothing," her mother insisted. "You've taken on so much."

There was a pause on the other side of the phone and Laura thought she heard a sniffle.

Oh, please, don't let her be crying, she thought.

"I've been working full-time since I was fifteen years old, but you're the best job I've ever done. I really mean that. I love you, honey."

"I love you, too." Laura covered her face with her hands. Her eyes stung.

All she wanted to do was crawl back into bed for the next twelve hours so she wouldn't have to think about what a terrible person—and disappointing daughter—she was. But she had history and she couldn't call attention to herself by skipping classes her first week. Willa was counting on her.

Laura grabbed her backpack and scooted out of Hub House, pausing only to toss Mrs. Pogue's latest care package—a throw pillow shaped like a leafy green vegetable with the words LETTUCE MAKE YOU THIN! embroidered across the front, accompanied by a short, frosty note "from Mother" as dictated to Emory—into the garbage.

As she walked, she kept her eyes trained on her feet. She was too depressed to play the "where's Caleb" game today.

"Willa!"

Laura twisted around as a hand jabbed her in the shoulder. Mr. Stade stood behind her, red-faced and breathless.

"I'm sorry about that," he said, coughing slightly, clearly embarrassed by his outburst. "I didn't mean to scare you or anything. I was just calling your name for a while—didn't you hear me?"

Great. She really had to start being more alert. It didn't matter what mood she was in; she couldn't jeopardize the plan. Too much was at stake.

She shrugged. "Uh, no. Sorry. I guess I'm just tired."

Mr. Stade fell into step beside her. "Well, you have been working overtime. I read through your proposal last night. It's excellent, Willa. I'm very impressed."

He was right—she *had* worked overtime. She'd started researching her first paper a few days ago and had worked incessantly for days. And if the compliment had come yesterday, she would have been elated. But after the conversation with her mother, she wasn't sure what to do with the praise.

"Thanks," she said, pushing an enthusiasm into her voice that she didn't feel.

"I don't think I've ever had a student hand in a topic only five days into the semester." He laughed, his eyebrows rising slightly from behind his round glasses. "The ambitious ones usually start around Columbus Day, but most leave all the work until Thanksgiving."

Laura shrugged. She knew she was supposed to be Willa Pogue, total academic slacker, but she'd already prepared an excuse. "A year ago, I wouldn't have bothered to write any papers at all, but I'm really trying to be organized now."

"What inspired this sudden change? I hope you don't mind my asking. It's just rare to see—especially so late in a school career."

Laura stared at her feet and forced herself to breathe. "Well, I guess I just got scared after the whole Shipley experience."

"Well, whatever the trigger, you should be very proud of

yourself." Mr. Stade cast her a sidelong glance. "It really is hard to believe you're the same person who attended Shipley, Willa. . . ."

Laura felt her insides twist. *Oh no.*

". . . Between this paper and the way you carry class discussions, you're performing like an honors student."

False alarm. "Thanks."

Relax, she ordered. *And cheer up. He's saying such nice things about a person he thinks is you.*

"Junior year is when the college pressure really starts up," Mr. Stade said as they climbed the stairs to Regan Hall. "Although I think students at a place like Fenwick feel college pressure when they start nursery school."

"Right," she agreed. Her stomach clenched. "It starts when you can hold a sippy cup."

"Do you know which schools you'll be looking at? Has your list changed at all since the sippy cup years?"

Laura had no idea how to answer. While it was true that *she'd* been obsessing about college, Willa had never even mentioned her post–high school plans. She'd barely talked about spring term, and that was less than six months away.

Mr. Stade's brow furrowed expectantly.

Laura sighed. It was just as well that she didn't know where Willa intended to apply. Because right now, Laura wouldn't have been able to sell it. She was sick of lying. The conversation with her mother still echoed in her head and, for now, she simply didn't want to add to her guilt. She would tell the truth. It was no big deal.

"UConn," she said simply. "Main campus."

Mr. Stade gave her a look filled with pity. "UConn is a good school," he said carefully. "I'm just a little surprised that you're not applying anywhere else. Maybe stretching just a bit."

Laura felt like kicking herself.

So much for telling the truth, she thought. *That's so not happening again.*

Laura's mind raced. This wasn't hopeless. *Just think.*

"Well, I did just get my act together," she said, pushing out a laugh. "I mean, you should see my transcript. It's about as pleasant as a stroll through a minefield."

"I know you've had a rough couple of years," he said. "But you could always apply and see what happens. Schools really do like to see an improvement, and you've done a real one-eighty, you know. If you're worried about recommendations, you can always come to me."

"Thanks," said Laura, shifting her weight from side to side. "That's, um, amazing of you."

She glanced toward Regan Hall longingly. *Now can we please go to class and talk about the McKinley assassination in peace?* she thought. *Please?*

"I have a friend at Kenyon," Mr. Stade said as he pulled open the door. "It's an excellent school."

Laura had never even heard of Kenyon.

"I really need to talk things over with my parents," she said. She tried to push the right amount of doubt into her voice without sounding rude. "We, uh, haven't really had a chance to talk much. They've been a little unhappy with me—with my grades."

They were at Mr. Stade's desk now, watching the other

students pour in around them. A few lined up behind her to speak with Mr. Stade before the bell rang.

"Well, I'm happy to help if I can."

Laura slid into a chair. Willa would *kill* her if she applied anywhere for her. That was definitely *not* part of the plan.

"Hey, Willa. Have you gotten your PhD yet?" Caleb dropped his long, lean body into the chair next to her and swiped his hand across his face as he issued a yawn that grew into a smile.

How did he always manage to sneak up on her like that? she wondered. And how did he always manage to look so good?

Even this morning, with a severe case of bed head and two different socks, Caleb looked good. She sighed. The guy just couldn't make himself look unattractive. It really was hopeless. Tarred and feathered, he'd still be cute. Fuzzy, but cute.

Be strong, Laura thought. *You need to kick the Caleb Blake habit.*

"I thought I'd settle for my master's this month. How about you?"

"Nah. I'm all or nothing." His cheeks had color today, she noticed. He'd probably been outside, playing Frisbee or something. Or had he been with Courtney?

Stop. She couldn't let her mind wander this way. *Don't go down that path. Just stop.*

This is history class, Laura said to herself. *That's my mantra. This is history class. Just do your work.*

The bell rang and Mr. Stade led the class into their discussion of Leon Czolgosz, the anarchist who shot President McKinley.

Laura breathed a sigh of relief. She was home free.

161

The problem was, history class lasted only fifty minutes. At which point, Laura returned to her semi—okay, fully—obsessed state and Caleb returned to Courtney, whose impatient little body greeted him in the hallway after *every* class.

As the bell signaled the end of the period, Caleb stood over Laura, smiling.

"Hey, what are you up to now? Do you have class?"

"Uh, no," Laura said, eyeing the doorway, half expecting Courtney Wilton to come barreling through blasting an Uzi, maybe two. "I have a free."

Caleb dropped his bag over his shoulder so that the strap cut across his body on a diagonal. "Me too. Want to get some food?"

Laura's toes curled. *I shouldn't do this*, she thought.

One meal. A snack. Was a snack really breaking the rules?

"I—"

"Willa, can I talk to you for a minute? I have some comments on your outline."

Laura knew she should either thank Mr. Stade or kill him, but she settled for a tiny nod instead. She turned back to Caleb.

"Sorry," she said.

"Another time." As he started to move off, something inside her crashed.

Stay, she begged. The word flashed through her head in bold neon. *Please stay*.

As if on cue, Caleb stopped and turned. "I, uh, well—I've been meaning to check in with you for a while. You know, see how you're liking it here and everything."

Laura laughed. "Your mom's been bugging you again, right?"

He shook his head. "No, nothing like that," he said. "This time it was my idea. Listen, I'll let you talk to Stade, okay?"

Laura watched him walk away. And as she trudged up to the desk, she knew, beyond a reasonable doubt, that she definitely wanted to kill her history teacher.

24

Agreeable manners are very frequently the fruits of a good heart, and then they will surely please, even though they may lack somewhat of graceful, courtly polish.
—*A Manual of Etiquette, with Hints on Politeness and Good Breeding*
Daisy Eyebright

Willa answered the wail of her alarm clock with a long, low groan. Another day. Another dirty house. More bizarre secrets to unearth.

She grabbed her phone off the bedside table.

```
boardgirl: u up?
lubespecial: am now. u do know it's 3
hours earlier here?
boardgirl: sorry. am just having
trouble getting up. say something
that will motivate, ok?
lubespecial: money. goodnight.
```

Willa shoved the phone under her pillow and pulled the covers over her head. "I can't do it," she moaned loudly. "I just can't."

Angie's large frame appeared in the doorway. She was already dressed for work in her blue Dr. Pool jumper.

"I heard you screaming from the kitchen. You sick, Professor?"

Willa propped herself up on her elbows. "I'm okay," she said, touched by the display of concern. "Don't worry."

"Oh, good. I thought maybe it was all the Jelly Bellies we ate last night."

"No, nothing like that." Willa paused for a few seconds, debating whether or not to continue. She and Angie had hung out a lot over the past week, but the two had never really had a serious conversation. She shrugged. "I guess I'm just a little sick of work."

Angie clucked sympathetically. "You've got the hard job, Professor. It's like I say to Dad, I don't know how you and your mom do it. It's what I always say."

"You do?" Willa looked up, startled. "But you work longer hours than I do. Plus, you get all those emergency calls."

Angie swatted at the air with an oversized hand, like Willa's comment was a fly buzzing around her head. "That's no big deal. My work keeps me *outside* the house. It's once you go inside that things start getting really weird, right?"

Willa bit her lower lip.

How had Angie done it? In just a few words, she'd summed up Willa's entire week—and the way she'd been feeling.

Willa sank back against the headboard and let a thicket of blond hair fall across her face. It was so easy to write the girl off as a clod—an overgrown townie who tucked her brain into her biceps. Willa herself had been guilty of issuing the stereotype—even before the two girls had met.

But life with Angie was definitely not the rough and bruising affair she'd anticipated. Angie had so completely surpassed these low expectations—she helped around the house, cooked and seemed to have a direct handle on Willa's every mood—that Willa was ashamed to have even thought them in the first place.

Maybe I should come clean and tell her about the switch, she thought. *She could handle it.*

On the other hand, Angie might get angry. Her hugs were painful enough. Willa couldn't even imagine what the girl's reaction to bad news might be.

Besides, what if Angie told her dad? Benji would probably feel like he had to tell Laura's mom. Then Laura would get into trouble. At the very least her mother would probably have to leave Miami. And it would be all Willa's fault.

That settled it. No matter how guilty she felt, Willa had to stick to the plan.

She pushed her hair out of her eyes.

"That's it, exactly," she said. "And I have to go to work now but I'm dreading it. I can't deal."

"Listen, you gotta remind yourself that it's just a job—you know? Don't let anyone drag you down. 'Cause no matter what, those families aren't your family. Your mom, my dad and me. We're what's real."

Willa's eyes filled with surprise tears. Angie was wrong—sweet, but wrong. Willa had no place in this reality. Her situation here was temporary—a short-term rental at best.

The Youngs were the only family on Willa's cleaning roster whose house didn't qualify as a mansion. They owned a redbrick split-level on one of Greenwich's more modest streets.

For Willa, it was love at first sight.

Even though no one was home—Mr. and Mrs. Young worked full-time and their two small children attended the local elementary school—Willa decided that it was impossible for the place to ever truly be empty. It was just way too happy-looking, too alive.

Every crumb, every color, every tiny imperfection—and there were a lot—fascinated her. As she moved through the rooms, her mind soaked up each detail as thoroughly as a paper towel passing over spilled milk. She wanted it all: the goofy family photos displayed in cheap, store-bought frames; the scattered toys; and the disorganized array of kids' artwork that hung just about everywhere—from windows, doors and walls.

A greatest hits medley of Young family moments was rapidly unfolding in her head: tickle sessions, bedtime stories, mac and cheese dinners. They were all there, as if the memories were her own.

This is what a family should look like, she thought.

An image of Pogue Hall blew through her like a gust of wind stamping out a flame. She shivered.

Of all the homes on her roster, Pogue Hall was by far the gloomiest. Sure, she hadn't discovered any bizarre secrets like the weirdness over at the Mortimers' or the Watsons'. Life at Pogue Hall was dull; its closets contained no skeletons, just cleaning products and clothing.

In a way, though, that only made the place seem worse. The whole mansion—Willa's childhood home—was simply void.

Willa glanced around the Youngs' kitchen. Three long green lights dangled from the ceiling, casting a bright, happy glow against the pale yellow walls and white-tiled floors.

There was a note for her on the counter from Mrs. Young:

Hi Laura - Running late this morning (what else is new!?). Hope you had a great summer - we missed you although had lots of fun with my parents at the Cape. Now that it's back to work/school we're so glad you're here—what a lifesaver you are! No special instructions—just do your thing and please help yourself to anything in the fridge that isn't moving! Thanks again!

Emily

The note had been written with two different pens and was covered with crumbs. Willa imagined Mrs. Young scribbling furiously while the chaos of breakfast rose around her. She read the note three times before wiping it off and slipping it into her pocket.

Snapping on a pair of gloves, Willa grabbed a bucket. She was determined to clean this house like it had never been cleaned before. She'd get out stains. She'd sweep and mop *behind* the refrigerator and couch. She'd be the Lance Armstrong of maids.

She didn't care that she'd never met this family before. She didn't care that they seemed more than satisfied with the service Laura and her mother had provided up to this point. She didn't care.

Because she was, after only one day, addicted to this house; to its smell; its overstuffed furniture; the sense of warm completion that washed over her as soon as she passed through the front door. She could handle the other houses, with all their strange little secrets, so long as she had this one.

25

Have you ever been ashamed of your
white socks, ashamed of your white shorts
or ashamed of your tights?
—*Oxydol Detergent*

It was a beautiful day. The sun was shining. The birds were chirping.

And Laura Melon was tucked away in a dormitory basement, doing laundry.

Over the past few weeks her desk had become a guilt magnet, housing her mother's postcards, which arrived on an almost daily basis, care of Willa. The scenes were always different: sunset beaches, coral reefs, or the infamous "My mom went to Florida and all I got was this lousy postcard." Laura could easily picture her mother shopping at the tourist stands, proudly selecting a different snapshot for every day. The image always caused Laura's stomach to seize—even before she turned the card over and absorbed her mother's neat, slanted print and cheerful message.

Laura kept them locked in the back of her desk drawer, safe and completely out of sight, but just knowing they were around was unsettling.

As if that weren't bad enough, the top of her desk now served as a breeding ground for college viewbooks. Kenyon, Wesleyan, Smith, Middlebury, Bates—every time she turned her head a glossy new brochure seemed to appear.

Laura had accepted the first information packet—from Kenyon—graciously. Unfortunately, despite her best attempts at enthusiasm, Mr. Stade had sensed a hesitance in her voice.

"Some people don't like Ohio," he'd suggested, scanning her face closely for clues.

"Not me. I love Ohio. I *really* love Ohio," she'd sworn, even though she had no opinion about the state whatsoever.

A week later Mr. Stade had handed her another pile of viewbooks. "You should be thinking of a large variety. I'm sure your parents will agree—once they get back from their trip."

Laura had responded with as much fake excitement as she could muster. What choice did she have?

Laura had managed to dodge Mr. Stade so far, but she'd have to read the books sooner or later.

It wasn't like she didn't want to learn about the schools, either. She'd even reached for the books a few times but had stopped herself. She'd been through this before, last fall. The conversation with Mr. Atkins—the one she'd tried so hard to forget—kept scratching through her brain like a Brillo pad on fine china. She couldn't apply, couldn't risk falling in love with yet another school—another Fenwick—she could never afford. (The burden of a loan was out of the question, and if she was turned down for a scholarship she'd be crushed.) What would she do then—scour the campuses for a look-alike willing to swap lives for four years? Right.

So Laura had done her very best to avoid the brochures altogether. She studied, went to classes and meals and basically tried to stick to a business-as-usual routine. It was the original plan, after all.

Still, no matter how hard she tried, the stupid viewbooks overwhelmed her tiny room, swallowing everything in it—including her. And now they were tormenting her. They knew who she was, that she didn't belong.

The stupid information packets were driving her crazy.

And just when Laura was sure things couldn't get any weirder, a third, equally bizarre problem had her running straight down to the laundry room.

She'd been accosted by Jenna Palmer.

Laura had been on her way to class when the dorm advisor had popped up out of nowhere.

"Hey, you." Jenna wore her usual uniform: overalls, bare feet. She flashed Laura the peace sign. "Listen, Willa. I've been meaning to talk to you. Do you have a minute?"

"No, not really. I have English lit."

"Great, great. This'll only take a second." Jenna swept Laura into the student lounge and sat cross-legged on the far edge of a sofa cushion. "So listen, Willa, what's happening?" she said. "We never talk. Why is that?"

Laura shrugged. *Because you say things like 'we never talk.'*

"Listen, I wanted to speak with you because, well, to be honest, I'm just a little concerned about your lack of involvement so far this year."

Laura blinked. "Huh?" Inside, her mind tripped into full panic mode. Had Jenna spoken with Mr. Stade? Was this about the whole college thing? Maybe she'd run into him at some faculty meeting? Had she called the Pogues? And what was *wrong* with the teachers at Fenwick? Didn't they have lives of their own?

"You've been here, what, almost six weeks? And you haven't gone to one dorm function or meeting—and we've had several since the term started," Jenna explained. "It wouldn't bother me except that I don't ever see you leave your room or socialize—not with anyone on your floor or anyone period. You seem very isolated."

"Um, I'm not sure what you mean," Laura said, speaking slowly. "I go to all my classes."

Jenna blew out a long, low sigh. "Willa, school—especially a place like Fenwick—is so much more than just class and studying," she said, clearly disheartened by Laura's profound ignorance. "There are clubs, teams, fund-raisers. You get so much from just going down to the student center on a Friday night and bonding with your classmates." Jenna's forehead puckered with concern. "I know you've had some trouble in the past and you're under a lot of pressure. But you need to get out more. School can't just be about the work. The pressure will get to you."

"I guess I just got a little too carried away," Laura said, trying hard to sound earnest. "You know, a little too stressed. I promise to make more of an effort." She'd have to be sure to take more walks in the future or something—anything to show the dorm advisor she was "circulating."

Jenna placed her palm over her chest. "So glad to hear that,

Willa. You've got to put yourself out there like you really want to *be* out there." Then, as if suddenly remembering that she was a hippie, Jenna cleared her throat and added, "It totally brings me down to have to have these talks, you know, but I thought it was important. People really do pick up on negative energy—don't you think?"

And so here she was. Laura lugged her duffel bag and economy-sized bottle of detergent toward the dark, moist basement and sighed. It certainly wasn't the most picturesque spot on campus, but after the viewbooks and Jenna Palmer, it felt like heaven. Doing laundry was the perfect way to take a little breather, stop time for a bit. She needed to get out of her room and clear her head, but the campus really wasn't the place to do that. She'd just end up searching for—

"Hey, Willa."

Caleb was there, standing over a row of washing machines. A strange lightness spread over Laura, like her laundry bag had become a helium balloon.

Of all places to see him. He always caught her by surprise.

"Hi," she said, pushing her bag into the room. "It's, uh, nice to see you." She was dying to ask him why he was in her laundry room instead of his own, but she couldn't think of a way to ask that didn't sound rude.

"Almost all the machines in my dorm are broken," Caleb explained as if he'd just read her mind. "And the ones that do work are being used." He hoisted an overstuffed bag onto a closed machine and grimaced. "I was gonna wait, but it's getting kind of desperate."

Laura did a quick mental rundown of her appearance and tried not to cringe. She was wearing sweatpants and the same shirt she'd slept in and hadn't brushed her hair.

It's not my fault, she thought defensively. *He's not supposed to be here.*

Okay, so she wasn't looking her best. That was probably a good thing. She wasn't, after all, here to flirt with him.

And then there was the Courtney issue.

At the mere thought of Caleb's girlfriend, Laura scanned the room. She half expected the tiny, sour-faced girl to pop up from behind a washer-dryer, firing a bleach-filled squirt gun.

But the room was empty. She and Caleb were alone.

A thrill. She definitely felt a thrill. But there was an after-taste of guilt.

She could say she'd forgotten something in her room, then not come back. She could say she had to make a phone call. She could—

Caleb leaned over and picked up her bag, dropping it on the machine next to his. The clean, soapy smell of his hair filled her head.

"Relax," he said. "Stay awhile."

She could, Laura realized, also do her laundry and stop reading so much into every tiny thing. She *had* promised her dorm advisor that she'd make an effort to be more social.

Laura opened her laundry bag and peered inside. *Ugh.* She wondered if there was any way she could get her laundry done and talk to Caleb yet simultaneously shield his eyes from the sight of her dirty clothes—especially her underwear.

Admittedly, it was a tall order.

Oh, get over it, she thought, grabbing a handful of clothes. *He's definitely seen worse.*

"Thanks," she said as she separated her whites and darks. "I was going a little stir-crazy in my room."

"I warned you, right? The workload is tough." Caleb slid his bag over so she'd have more room. "I thought I'd have it easy, being a senior, but so far no such luck." He tossed some clothes into the washer, then turned to her. "But you like it here, right?"

"I really do," she said. Then, thinking of the viewbooks piled high on her desk and her conversation with Jenna Palmer, she added: "It's, uh, a little stressful, but I'm really happy."

Laura shifted her weight. Caleb's expression had changed and it caught her off guard. His eyes were suddenly intense, bright and alert. He was studying her.

Her heart started to pound.

"You know," he said slowly, "you really don't have to do that."

Laura followed his gaze. Her hands, programmed for laundry, had somehow worked their way across machines, to Caleb's pile. While she was talking, she'd been treating a nasty grass stain on his soccer shorts (Spray 'n Wash stain stick, then wash warm).

"Oh, I'm really sorry!" she said, releasing the shorts as if they'd bitten her. "I, uh, I guess I'm sort of a neat freak."

Caleb laughed. "I wish I had that problem." He cleared his throat and looked up. "Oh, hey, have you started studying for Stade's class?"

Laura shook her head. Their history class was in a mini-uproar over their first test, which was next Friday. "I was going to start this week."

"I was thinking maybe we could study together." He grinned. "I mean, that's assuming I can get my whites as white as yours. I wouldn't want to embarrass you or anything."

Laura laughed, but inside her head the alarm bells were already sounding. An accidental meeting in the laundry room was one thing. Making plans was another.

I have to say no, she thought. She had to thank him but insist that she *always* studied alone. Or something. It wouldn't be hard: *No thanks. No thanks. Maybe another time.*

Laura opened her mouth and, in a voice she'd never in a million years have recognized as her own, said, "Sounds great. What are you doing later?"

26

Exercise is unquestionably one of the very
best means for the preservation of health;
but its real importance is unknown, or
but too lightly considered by the majority
of females.
—*The Lady's Guide to Perfect Gentility*
Emily Thornwell

Angie barged into Willa's room early Sunday morning.

"Rise and shine, Professor!" she shouted. "I got a surprise for you!"

Willa yawned. "What is it?" she said.

Angie beamed. "If I told you, it wouldn't be a surprise, would it? Now, we got to be on the road in forty minutes, so get up. I'm cooking light—bagels and cream cheese."

Willa sat up. "What's the surprise for?"

Angie shrugged. "Remember when you had that rough week a while back? Well, that's when I thought this up. Now come on—get moving. You really don't want to be late. We're taking Yellow Thunder out today."

Willa hopped out of bed. This really was big. Angie's car had recently suffered some sort of meltdown and ever since, she'd been driving it only on special occasions.

The question was: Would Angie and Willa's definition of "special occasion" match?

Willa frowned as she grabbed a clean towel from the linen closet and headed to the bathroom. It didn't matter, she decided. Whatever activity Angie chose for them today, she would be gracious. She would force herself to have fun. Because Angie was sweet. And she'd planned the whole day for her.

Less than two hours later, as Angie parked Yellow Thunder outside the Thompson Speedway, Willa's confidence faltered.

"NASCAR?" Willa asked, incredulous. "We're going to a NASCAR race?"

"Not just any race," Angie declared proudly. "*The Super Dirt Series—Dodge 500*. Tickets are in the glove compartment."

Willa forced her lips into a smile. "Wow. Uh, thanks, Angie. That's fantastic. I've never been to—"

Angie snorted. "Course you haven't, Professor! That's why I knew you had to come. You're gonna *love* it. Wait'll you see the speed—it's amazing. C'mon, let's go inside. I'll explain everything, but it's real easy to follow." Her eyes widened. "Ah, there he is!" She pointed across the parking lot. Glenn was leaning against his car, but when he saw them, he waved.

"He got here early, to try and get another ticket in our row," Angie explained. Her wide forehead wrinkled. "He might not have been able to—most years the Dirt Series sells out way early."

Willa unfastened her seat belt and trailed after Angie. "You know, you didn't have to take me. I mean, I'm sure it would've been more fun for you guys to take someone who really knows about racing."

Angie grinned as they walked toward Glenn. "We wanted to take you. You needed this." She opened her arms wide as the raceway came into view. "Besides, how can you not love this? It cheers you up instantly, doesn't it?"

Willa knew she was being a baby, but she actually felt a little sorry for herself. She couldn't help it. Two days off a week, that was all she got. And now she was wasting one of them at the track, like a bookie. No, it was worse than that. At least bookies made money on stuff like this.

Sports bored Willa. She could never keep the rules straight and she never cared if her team lost or won. All her life, gym teachers were constantly screaming at her, furious that she'd "traveled" in a basketball game or "used her hands" during soccer practice. She never understood what the big deal was. Everyone loved to travel. Hands were pretty cool too.

After years of athletic misery, she failed to see how this experience was going to turn her into a superjock. To top it off, Willa had that attention-span problem—as in, she had no attention span.

The situation was hopeless.

How long does one of these things last? she wondered.

Glenn was smiling broadly. He held up his ticket. "Nice, right?"

Angie let out a loud whoop as they moved through the tailgaters. "It's, like, right next to us. How'd you swing that?"

He laughed. "Luck, I guess." He looked at Willa. "So, are you psyched for your first NASCAR experience?"

"It's pretty fantastic so far, right?" said Angie as they pushed toward their seats.

Willa felt guilty for being such a spoiled brat. Angie and Glenn were so nice. And so enthusiastic.

"It's excellent," she said, trying to sound excited. "Thanks so much."

Willa looked around. She was surprised by the variety of cars in the parking lot. She'd expected a sea of monster trucks, driven by sleazy men with slicked-back hair, wearing mesh tank tops. And there were some of those. But there were also lots of normal-looking people. And families with small kids, running eagerly toward the track, hoping for a glimpse of their favorite driver.

"Wow, they really do pack it in here," Willa said.

"Oh, sure," Glenn agreed matter-of-factly. "I had to get up at six to wait in line for tickets."

Willa reminded herself to act extra enthralled once the race started.

Shoving her hands under her thighs, she tried not to fidget. She stifled a yawn but forced herself to keep her eyes glued to the track. She'd sat through so much worse—boring classes, parent and teacher lectures—she could deal with NASCAR. This really wasn't all that bad.

"Oh, oh, good!" Angie exclaimed. "They're starting. I'm so psyched. Professor, you're going to love this!"

Willa held her eyes tight on the track. If she looked away she was done for.

She watched as men wearing brightly colored snowsuits defied all laws of spatial relations by folding themselves into tiny high-gloss cars. It looked kind of cool, the way the seats conformed snugly to each driver's body, effortlessly hugging his frame.

"*Gentlemen, start your engines!*" trumpeted a loud, low baritone. Willa jumped as a thunderous roar filled the speedway and the cars lurched forward. The crowd went wild.

"What's the big thing in NASCAR?" Willa asked, more out of boredom than any genuine interest.

"Huh?" Angie was staring at the track, totally captivated.

"I mean, in football there's the Super Bowl. In baseball there's the World Series. What's the big thing for NASCAR?"

"They all want the Nextel Cup," Glenn explained. His eyes were also trained on the speedway. "Big money. Millions. Lots of endorsements and stuff, too. The usual."

Willa had never heard of the Nextel Cup. Feeling oddly excluded, she turned back to the cars. They were definitely loud, but there was also a kind of grace to them, in the way they slipped around the circle like figure skaters on ice. She had to admit, it was kind of cool.

Red, she thought as her fingers curled around an imaginary steering wheel. *I think I'd want a red car.*

Willa liked to drive. Other than the convenience factor, though, she'd never really thought much about driving—or cars. But suddenly, that seemed strange to her. The world was, after all, car-obsessed.

What makes it go so fast? She eyed a bright orange car with the number five stenciled on the door. *Could an ordinary car—the fancy ones maybe—drive just as fast?*

"Hey," she said. "What's that thing in the front of the cars—below the front bumper?"

Angie squinted. "Oh, that's the—*Come on, Stewart! Don'tcha wanna light your wheels!*— Sorry, that's the valance. It changes your downforce."

Willa paused. "Uh, what's downforce?"

Angie pounded Willa's shoulder like she was clapping out a fire. "Told you you'd love it here! It's the best, right? Okay, let's see, downforce is what gives you your tire grip, see? You need it to corner. But you have to be careful because too much downforce can mean too much drag. And that slows you down, right? Too much drag's a drag."

Angie dissolved into a fit of cackling snorts while Willa gingerly rotated her bruised arm.

"Now, this driver I like, Tony Stewart," Angie continued. "His car's number twenty. See it there? He's won two championships in the last four years."

Glenn grinned. "Don't listen to her, Laura," he teased. "She just likes him 'cause she thinks he's cute."

"That's not true!" Angie laughed. "Okay, maybe it's a little true. But he's also a great driver."

Willa pointed at the track. "But he's way in the back."

"Nah. Don't let that fool you. They do five hundred laps. I was just joking around before. It's the time that counts. It's too early to tell."

Five hundred laps? Willa turned back to the track as the cars zoomed off the course into tiny stalls. Good thing they were going so fast.

"What's going on now?"

"Those are pit stalls." Angie pointed to the uniformed figures zipping up and down the cars. "When the driver takes a car in for a pit stop, he drives in there so his crew can do some adjustments. You know, change the tires or whatever."

Willa watched as the crews ran up and down the cars, zipping back and forth. It was amazing how synchronized their movements were. From far away, they almost looked like they were dancing.

She stared, mesmerized, until every car drove back out onto the track.

"What do the flags mean?" she asked, craning her neck forward.

"Oh, well, it's pretty much like regular traffic lights, really. Green is go, yellow is slow down and hold your position behind the pace car . . ."

Willa listened, her eyes glued to the multicolored cars zipping around the course. She kept waiting for her body to betray her: for her legs to squirm, her mind to wander, her stomach to issue its trademark snarl.

But the only thing that moved was Willa's pulse, which was suddenly in competition with the speeding cars below. It sprinted to new levels, leaving MySpace and Lubé Special behind. This was something completely singular, an excitement Willa owned completely. It left her red-faced and breathless, like she herself was racing five hundred laps.

She didn't mind, though. She embraced the heat. She reveled in the sweat.

Because for the first time in her life, Willa Pogue was interested in something.

And for Willa, something was no small thing.

27

Where the heart is
—Procter & Gamble Cleaning Products

Showered, shampooed, blown dry (an extremely rare event) and reoutfitted for the thousandth time, Laura Melon was ready.

It hadn't been easy to surpass her normal, everyday look without appearing too dressed up or made up. Laura didn't have any experience on the subject of study dates.

Not that this was a date date, of course.

Standing in front of her full-length mirror, Laura studied her reflection. Her hair hung loose around her shoulders and her jade eyes were sharp and clear. She wore a little mascara and lip gloss, and a spritz of body spray.

She had to keep things technical: the evening was just a study session. Okay. Fine. More specifically, it was a study session with an incredibly attractive member of the opposite sex *but* he *had a girlfriend* and his sole interest in her, Laura, was academic. He respected her mind—he thought of her as a great historian. A future PhD.

"And *that* is the most depressing thought I have ever had," she muttered to herself as she grabbed her backpack.

She pushed open the front door and stepped onto campus.

She'd been tempted to inform Jenna Palmer of her plans to score some "I'm socializing!" points but had decided against it. What better way to prove that she was socially impaired than by calling her dorm advisor to announce: *Hi, Jenna? I just wanted to let you know that I'm about to interact with a fellow student in a quasiextracurricular manner. . . .*

They'd arranged to meet in front of the library. As Laura approached the stone-columned building she noticed that Caleb was already there, bag slung loosely over his shoulder. He turned slightly.

His face looked . . . different. His features were tight and grim and, for the first time, she realized that he wasn't alone. Courtney was with him and she looked even more unhappy than usual.

The couple was engaged in a heated exchange.

Laura didn't know what to do. She could leave, of course. She wanted to leave. Only she couldn't. Her feet had grown roots.

She stood stock-still, staring at the arguing couple, until Caleb looked over and waved. The gesture seemed to be the final straw for Courtney, who turned on her heel and stormed off.

Caleb watched his angry girlfriend flounce across the quad, then walked over to where Laura was standing.

"Ready? I've been studying for a calculus exam all week so I might be kind of behind."

"Yeah," Laura said, shaking her head more out of confusion than anything else. "I don't want to pry, but Courtney looked pretty mad. Is everything okay?"

They walked into the library.

"No, but it'll blow over. Forget it."

In other words, butt out. "Okay."

Caleb was a little bit farther behind than she was; he'd been right. But he caught up to her in no time. Laura was amazed by how sharp he was, how quickly his mind could sift through information and zero in on what was important.

"Okay, so I think we should definitely go over the sinking of the battleship—the *Maine*," Caleb suggested, his head bent low over his notebook. "You know one of the essay questions will be about the motives for war."

"Definitely," Laura agreed. "And there's also going to be something about the Platt Amendment, so we should probably reread the section about long-term effects."

"You're right." Caleb flipped ahead a few pages in their history text and then looked up at her. "You know," he said slowly, "Courtney's jealous of you."

Laura's head jerked up so quickly, she pulled a muscle in her neck. "Ow. What?"

Caleb shrugged. "She's always been kind of jealous in general, but now that you're here she's kind of gone off the deep end." He smiled warily. "It took me forever to convince her that I didn't need a personal escort to and from Stade's class."

"I don't get it," Laura said. "I mean, that's kind of paranoid. We just have class together." She twirled her pen nervously. "Well, I guess there is the family connection. Is that why she's jealous? Because our parents are friends?"

"She thinks we have some sort of thing going on."

"It's called U.S. history! Besides that I barely see you."

"Why is that?" he asked.

Wait, was he flirting with her? Was he *leaning* toward her? It was hard to tell; she felt dizzy all of a sudden.

Laura cleared her throat. "I've been, you know, busy, I guess," she said. She didn't recognize her own voice. "I have so much work and I'm new and I'm, uh, trying not to screw up anymore."

Caleb's laugh broke the tension. "Too bad we're not studying the Civil War. Honest Abe would be proud of you."

Perfect, Laura thought. She was exactly where she wanted to be. The room no longer had wings. Everything had fallen neatly back into place.

Everything, of course, except her heart. The tiny, aching muscle felt like a cushion in her chest, each of Caleb's friendly smiles a pin.

The tricky part of it was: She couldn't remove them.

Even if she died of internal bleeding.

28

You have no business buying a Ferrari of any sort or, really, any other Flashy Sports Car. And there is no excuse whatsoever for driving a car that has any Essential Parts either missing or affixed to the car avec Duct Tape.
—*More Things You Need to Be Told*
Lesley Carlin, Honore McDonough Ervin,
Etiquette Grrls

boardgirl: if u cld hav 1 dream come tru - wut wld it b?
lubespecial: tuf 1. 4 yrs wanted 2 go bak in time and hav 80s Van Halen beg me 2 share spotlight w/ David Lee Roth but hav just about given up on time travel. And VH. Nu stuf suks so bad, even 80s are tainted.
boardgirl: so, wut's nu dream come tru scenario?
lubespecial: 2 meet u.

```
boardgirl: am serious Lube
lubespecial: so am i.
lubespecial: r u there?
```

Willa had never been big on daydreams. Sure, she spaced out a lot. But spacing out and daydreaming were worlds apart. Spacing out required absolutely no thought or energy whatsoever. Daydreams involved a personal fantasy element. And Willa's fantasy life had always landed in one of two categories: food fantasies triggered by a stressful situation or event, and the more common "escape" dreams, in which Willa, playing a sort of selfish version of Harriet Tubman, set out to emancipate only herself from a variety of terrible oppressors—parents, teachers, faculty advisors.

And okay. *Occasionally*, a third fantasy—the "parent pleasers"—had cropped up. These involved the cliché straight-A report card or carload of "triple-p" (Pogue-approved, pretty and popular!) friends. In her most desperate moments, there might have even been some sort of dream about saving kittens from a burning building. Whatever.

The point was she didn't *have* a rich fantasy life. Even when she listened to Lubé Special, she never once envisioned herself actually playing the drums and running off with the band. She spent her time watching life from a distance, as a spectator. She never actually dreamed of accomplishing anything. Most of the time, she just went to sleep and slept. End of story. That was the way it had been for years.

NASCAR had changed everything.

It had been one week since the Super Dirt Series, with its squealing tires and bouncing mud flaps, and Willa had been doing nothing but racing. All day, every day. In her head.

The car was a fire-engine-red Monte Carlo, modeled after driver Jeff Gordon's. Her matching jumper stretched over her like icing on a sheet cake—and it looked twice as good, too. Her full name was written in cursive down her left arm. And the best part about this fantasy was: Willa never lost a race. Every time her brain screamed out: *Gentlemen, start your engines,* she was off, effortlessly peeling away from the pack. She was unstoppable. The Nextel Cup was hers for the taking!

It was all pretty juvenile. It was the type of fantasy sequence more suited to a four-year-old boy who slept in one of those plastic beds shaped like a race car. But she couldn't help it.

She wanted to *drive.* No, scratch that. She wanted more. She wanted to drive, change the oil *and* realign the wheels (only when necessary, of course. So far Laura's Chevy had been running smoothly, knock on wood).

And that was why this bright Saturday afternoon found Willa and Angie huddled under the hood of Yellow Thunder, poking around the car's somewhat sickly insides.

"I can't believe you wanted to do this, Professor." Angie was staring at her, confused. "The last time we tried, you couldn't get away fast enough."

"That was before NASCAR." Willa stared down at the Trans Am, hypnotized by the maze of tubes and wires. She wanted it all to make sense. Now.

Angie pounded her back. "I knew I should've taken you sooner!"

Willa rubbed her permanently battered shoulder. "I'm a sponge. Teach away."

"Wanna have lunch first? We haven't had anything since those eggs."

"After. I'm not hungry."

It was true, Willa suddenly realized. For the first time ever, she had no need for food.

"Wow, you're hard-core." Angie laughed as she leaned over the hood and rested a large foot on the front bumper. Yellow Thunder creaked loudly under the strain. "See, the first thing you need to know about is the ignition system, right?" She ran her index finger along the mess of hardware like she was sifting through a bowl of Chex Mix. "That's what produces the charge that gets carried by all these wires to the spark plugs. Here, you can actually see it when I turn the engine over. . . ."

Willa watched as the Trans Am sputtered to life, after only a mild protest. She breathed in the thick, stinky air and felt a thrill rise in her throat.

Angie cut the motor and climbed out of the car. "It doesn't sound right," she said, frowning. "Man, I *just* picked the car up from the shop. I'm so bummed."

"What's wrong?"

"I'm not sure." Angie looked almost weepy. "I know Yellow so well; I just kind of know when something's not right. The thing is, I spent so much on her fuel system I'm kind of broke."

"Can't you just do most of the work yourself?"

Angie shook her head mournfully. "Just the little stuff. You know, the tweaks. The huge jobs, I got to take her in for that."

She sighed as she stroked Yellow Thunder's hood affectionately. "I'm learning, but I guess I'm not learning fast enough."

As far as Willa was concerned, Yellow Thunder always sounded like it was one choke away from the scrapyard. But the last thing she wanted to do was hurt Angie's feelings. "Listen," she said, "start the car again. I'll listen more closely this time."

As Angie turned the car over, Willa squeezed her eyes shut and listened for the engine's low, hesitant grind.

It sounded as bad as usual. At first. And then she heard it.

Her eyes snapped open. "It's like a wheeze, right?" she said. "Like the car's got a cold?"

Angie pumped her head up and down enthusiastically. "Professor! You're a natural!"

Even though she knew Angie was just being nice, Willa felt pleased. She'd never been called a natural at anything. Maybe she'd finally found her niche. Willa thought back to the Super Dirt Series, how the pit crews had seemed so together—such a team. Maybe she could do something like that—if she really was a natural.

Willa stared down at the Trans Am's greasy interior. The Pogue family crest rose out of the tangle of plugs and cylinders.

It punched her squarely in the jaw.

A NASCAR pit crew. Willa Tierney Pogue. Right. Who was she kidding? She came from a long line of congressmen, financiers and scientists. She couldn't even imagine her mother *saying* NASCAR, let alone standing by while her only daughter pursued a career as a grease monkey. She doubted any Pogue had ever even filled a gas tank before. And what boarding school offered a class in popular mechanics? The whole idea was absurd.

Still, the Trans Am's hood was *already* popped. And Willa couldn't seem to tear her eyes away.

On the road of life there are passengers and there are drivers.

"Listen," Willa said, letting her head drop a little lower under the car's hood. "Let's find the source of the noise. Then maybe we can do some research and try to figure out how to fix the problem ourselves."

"Ya know, that's not a bad idea, Professor," Angie said, her face brightening. "It'd sure save me cash I don't have. Hey, and we could even call those guys, you know, the ones on that show—*Car Talk*? For help."

Willa's smile was wide and cocky. "Sure," she said. "But who says we'll need it?"

29

The only real replacement for the mop and bucket
—Swiffer WetJet Power Mop

"When was McKinley shot?"

"Wait, President McKinley was *shot*? You're joking."

"I can't believe Stade is doing this. He knows this is like the *worst* week. I have three papers due. *And* I'm taking around a prospective."

"Duh. That's why he's doing it. The teachers all load us up—"

"Wait. Did you say prospective? Is it a she? Is she hot?"

"Shut *up*. I have to study."

"Gotcha. Not hot."

Pre-exam stress was the same, more or less, at every school. Laura listened, amused, to the various conversations as they flew around the room. Personally, she could never understand what all the fuss was about. Everyone always acted like exams were wild and unpredictable—on a par with natural disasters or something. But exams were so easy to control. All you had to do was read, study, go to class and show up for the test.

Plus, exams had . . . concrete answers. Laura always found

that part oddly reassuring. It was everything else about life that freaked her out.

The voices escalated as the panic level rose. Laura had arrived a little early to squeeze some last-minute studying in, but it was impossible to concentrate with all the noise.

She glanced toward the doorway. And she saw them.

Caleb and Courtney were standing just outside the room.

Laura didn't wait to read the expressions on their faces or to have her insides twisted by their lovey-dovey looks. Courtney could direct her scowls elsewhere. And as for Caleb, well, Laura simply had no time for the perfect blue ocean of his eyes. She couldn't go wading. She couldn't even test the water.

I have a history exam to take, she thought, flipping through her notes. *I'm a serious student.*

She didn't look up—not even when Mr. Stade entered the room and began to distribute the tests. And not when Caleb followed a few minutes later, muttering an apology. She kept her eyes glued to her exam packet and sailed through question after question. The classroom melted away; time froze. When she completed the final essay, she was surprised to find that she'd finished fifteen minutes early.

She spent the rest of class reading over her test. Over and over again until the last bell rang. She followed a pack of students up to Mr. Stade's desk and dropped her exam onto the pile. *Please don't ask me about college*, she thought.

Caleb tossed his test onto the pile and turned to Laura. "You walking out?" He waved at Mr. Stade. "Or did you want to stay for another round?"

"Tempting, but no," she said. "I'm leaving."

Mr. Stade laughed. "I may or may not remember your insults while I'm grading. It could go either way."

"What'd you think?" Caleb said as they walked through the quad. "Not bad, right?"

"No surprises," Laura agreed. Then she added honestly, "Our study session really helped."

"It was great. Thanks for doing that." Caleb paused for a second, then motioned toward the dining hall. "Listen, tests always make me hungry. Do you want to get something to eat?"

"Won't Courtney get mad?" Laura didn't feel like dealing with any angry outbursts from paranoid girlfriends.

Caleb shrugged. "We broke up," he said without breaking his stride. His voice was maddeningly noncommittal. Even his walk—long, steady steps—was completely neutral.

Laura waited for Caleb to explain. She waited for him to say *something*.

He said nothing.

Caleb Blake was single. He was unattached. He was a bachelor (well, he'd always been a bachelor in the technical sense, but whatever). And as much as that thrilled her, it was also highly dangerous—toxic, even. Dinner with Caleb was not part of "the plan."

Willa would kill her.

On the other hand, they were entering the dining hall. What was Laura supposed to do? Wouldn't abruptly running off jeopardize the plan even more?

Laura saw Jenna Palmer waving out of the corner of her eye. That clinched it.

They sat outside, at one of the dark cedar picnic tables.

Laura brushed a few yellowing leaves off the surface and plopped her tray down.

"We can move inside if you're cold," Caleb offered. "I'm sorry, I should've asked before I led you out here."

"No. I like it. It'll be too cold soon. It's nice to be out here while we can."

Caleb yawned. "Sorry. It's not you. I've had a killer of a week. That history exam, calculus. Plus, I hear from colleges soon so I'm kind of stressed."

"Where did you apply?" she asked.

"Brown early decision," Caleb said. He opened a bag of potato chips and held the bag out to Laura. "But if I don't get in, I've got ten other schools to hear from. How about you? Junior year is when the whole mess starts up."

"Oh, I'm still putting together my list," she said lightly. "Listen, I know it's none of my business, but I saw you and Courtney talking right before history."

"I was wondering if you were going to ask about that." There was a smile in his voice.

"You can't blame me for being curious."

"Nope. I can't. Because you had a lot to do with why we broke up."

"I'm so sorry," she said. Her voice pushed out in quick, choppy beats. "If Courtney's jealous . . . I mean, I can explain that nothing happened. Let me explain, okay? It's the least I can do. I feel terrible. We only studied together that one time."

And then, just like that, Laura wasn't talking anymore. Caleb was leaning across the table, his hand pressed into the small of her back as his lips brushed gently against her own.

The kiss was soft at first, a question. But as Caleb's hand moved her body closer, the mood shifted. A current of excitement tripped through her, tickling as it rose from the soles of her feet to her throat. Laura stopped thinking. She was floating. She was gone.

"I wanted to break up," Caleb explained. "It's just until I met you, I didn't really know why. So, um, do me a favor. Don't apologize, okay?"

"Okay," Laura said.

Because if Willa saw what was happening right now, Laura would be apologizing for the next fifteen years.

30

People differ widely in their notions of veracity.
—The Secret of a Happy Home
Marion Harland

```
lubespecial: ru there?
lubespecial: ru there?
lubespecial: hit me bak wen u get a
chance, ok?
```

The cleaning caddy sailed down the glossy marble hallway, teetering slightly as it gained speed. From a few feet away, Willa considered her newly discovered stock car with a mix of pride and regret.

How had she lived in Pogue Hall all these years and not known how great the marble floor was for racing?

In only a few short days, Willa's car-obsessed mind had transformed all wheeled mechanisms into sleek racing machines. Vacuum cleaners, desk chairs and, of course, her very own cleaning caddy had all been tested, raced and rolled. Nothing was safe.

The cart came to a rolling stop against a long green curtain.

Willa caught up to it and gave it a shove in the opposite direction. The whole thing was totally immature. She'd be the first to admit it. But she was fine with that.

She glanced down at her watch. Yikes. She had a schedule to keep. Plus, the gardeners were arriving in an hour and a half. They never came into the house or anything, but still. Best to be out of the house by the time they showed up, just in case.

Thwack. The caddy crashed into the wall, sending various cleaning supplies flying.

I'm such an idiot, she thought, rushing over. *Of course that was going to happen.*

She deserved it, too. She'd been playing around instead of working. Just the sort of thing she'd promised Laura she *wouldn't* do. It was the sort of thing that could get them both caught. And Laura fired.

No, no it wasn't her fault, Willa decided firmly. Because this type of thing never would have happened over at the Youngs' house. She behaved herself at the Youngs'.

Pogue Hall, on the other hand, had no imprint whatsoever. Not even one thumb. The place had absolutely nothing to offer her during her brief respites from cleaning. There was no mac and cheese waiting in the fridge, no LEGO forts or dollhouses to marvel over, no signs of life at all. The closest thing to a human touch in the entire estate was her mother's thirty-year-old newspaper clippings, the yellowing pictures of a plastic debutante. And those were hardly the cornerstone of domestic bliss.

So *no*. Willa would *not* accept the blame here. Pogue Hall— this empty crypt of a place—had driven her to destruction.

Even so, guilt sliced through her. She couldn't stop it.

Okay, so she was building a weak defense. She was the one who'd crashed the cart, not the stupid house. *Fine*.

Willa slid her hand into her pocket and ran her fingers along Mrs. Young's most recent note. She kept all the Youngs' notes. She needed them. They helped her get through other, harder parts of her week.

Surveying the scene of the accident, Willa realized that the only casualty was a bottle of Murphy Oil Soap (Laura was right. It really *was* the best thing to use on wood paneling). Lucky break. She cleaned up the mess and ran down to the cellar for another jug.

"Hmm, Lemon Pledge, Clorox, Tide, Cascade," she muttered as she walked the aisles of the huge storage room, scanning the rows and rows of supplies. "Where's the stupid Murphy Oil? Please don't tell me we're out. This *so* figures."

And there it was. Shoved in a box behind the bottles of Clorox and Downy.

Bingo, Willa thought as she pulled down the dusty cardboard box. *I just saved myself a trip to the store*.

But the box housed no cleaning supplies whatsoever. Inside, coated in a thick film of grime, were a few old photos, a tightly rolled poster and, sealed in a plastic storage bag, a pair of pink ballet slippers.

Willa sifted through the pictures. They were all pretty much the same: black-and-whites featuring a beautiful young woman in a leotard standing at a barre, her long, lean body held in a fixed ballet pose.

My mother.

Slowly, she unrolled the poster. Her mother—dressed in a wide pink tutu and wearing entirely too much makeup—stared up at her. Scrolled across the bottom were the words: "Newport Ballet Academy presents *Coppélia*, starring Sibby Welles."

Willa's feet were firmly planted on the floor, she was sure of it. And yet, she was spinning. Or the room was. Something was making her dizzy—and not just a little nauseated. Willa extended her arm, using a box of Cascade as an anchor.

She turned her attention back to her mother.

Her mother was a dancer?

"How?" she asked the pictures. "You're a lady who lunches. You play tennis just so you can criticize everyone else's backhand. You're not even a Welles anymore, you're a Pogue."

The pictures gave her the silent treatment.

Willa sighed and flipped them over. They were all taken in 1976. *Coppélia* was performed then, too.

Okay. At least she had a date. 1976. Her mother had been seventeen.

So, Sibby Welles Pogue was more than a pretty face who "took the Newport deb scene by storm." She was a ballerina.

Was she really amazing? Willa wondered. *Maybe she quit when she got married, because she wanted a quieter life?*

Still, Willa had an odd feeling that dancing must have meant something to her mother—at least at one point. Otherwise, she wouldn't have saved any memorabilia. And then there was her silence on the subject. That said a lot too.

There was definitely a story there. The crypt finally had a story.

Carefully, Willa packed up the box and placed it back on the shelf, exactly where she had found it, amid the bleach and fabric softener.

Lifting her hands over her head, she turned and leapt out the door.

31
See your world in high definition
—Bounty Paper Towels

Laura's new favorite word was "amend." As in: "I've amended the plan. Boyfriends are permitted."

Correction. The plan had amended itself.

It all felt so natural, as natural as that very first kiss.

That kiss.

The kiss had changed everything. It was like she'd been listening to the world through headphones, set at volume five. And then Caleb had come along and twisted the dial up to ten. Suddenly, Laura's days were lined with sound. She was listening to life in stereo.

Laura walked around campus, ecstatic. She looked forward to little things, like eating lunch and studying in the library and doing her laundry. Because little things were all a part of life and, during those moments, she loved life. No, it was more than that. She looked *forward* to life. And a life with Caleb in it was so perfect—so amazing—that when they walked together, she actually felt taller. Sometimes she even checked her feet, to make sure they were still on the ground.

It was an entirely new sensation.

And then there were moments when doubt clouded everything. Like a storm cloud rolling in over an outdoor reception, it always reared its head at the most inopportune moments. One minute Laura and Caleb would be sitting in history class, mid-debate; the next she'd be frozen, chilled by the voice in her head as it hissed, *You're a liar. Your whole relationship is built on a lie. He has no idea who you are.*

The worst part of all was that Laura knew the voice was right.

It wasn't that she didn't want to be honest. She did. She was dying to, only she kept chickening out. During the day they never seemed to have a second alone—class and homework always interfered. And then of course, every other time of day, she had to deal with how cute Caleb was. It simply wasn't a fair fight.

Still, she'd made a valiant effort. She'd even risked suspension by sneaking into his dorm room late one Saturday night. All the way over to his room, she'd rehearsed her lines and sworn she'd keep her eyes glued to the rug.

She'd climbed through the window, upsetting a pile of Caleb's books in the process. She started in immediately before she lost her nerve.

"I'm-not-who-you-think-I-am-I'm-different-sorry-about-the-books," she announced, breathless from her cross-campus sprint.

Caleb grabbed her hand and pulled her the rest of the way into the room. "Look. Relax. I mean, I'm glad you're here, but you don't have to say that."

Laura blinked. "Huh?"

"Willa, I know what you're trying to say." He twisted her hair slowly around his finger. "I know about Shipley. Our parents are friends, remember?" He looked at her. "I don't care about any of that. I know who you are. The real you. Who you were before—and what you did—it doesn't matter."

Who could resist a speech like that?

So she pressed her face against Caleb's chest, where it was always warm, and the clouds passed. She was being selfish. And it felt good.

The next day, she slipped on Willa's jeans and a gray cashmere sweater, swept a brush through her hair, whisked some blush across her cheeks. Then she grabbed her jacket and went off to meet Caleb.

He was sitting on a bench in front of the dining hall. When he saw her walking toward him, he stood. "Hey. You should've stayed last night. I couldn't sleep."

"Really? You wanted me to stay so you could sleep?" Laura teased. "Interesting." She turned toward the dining hall. "So, what are you thinking? Two by the window or should we just eat at the bar?"

Caleb shook his head. "Neither. Let's split."

"What are you talking about?"

He was walking away from her now, heading toward the wrought-iron gates that separated the campus from the town of Old Saybrook.

"Wait, where are you going?"

"Come see," he shot over his shoulder.

Laura trailed after him but when she saw the yellow cab

standing a few feet away, a cold anxiety swept through her. *He got the wrong impression last night and he's taking me to a Motel 6.*

That was Laura's first thought. But then she looked at Caleb, standing at the cab. He was holding the door open for her, a cute, eager grin spread across his face. And suddenly she knew that whatever he had planned did not involve a fleabag motel. No way.

She slid inside the car and fastened her seat belt.

"Where are we going?"

Caleb stretched his arm lightly across her shoulder. His blue eyes twinkled. "It's a surprise."

Laura leaned back against his chest and tried to step into the role of curious, excited girlfriend ("I want to know! Tell me!"). But as the cab drove farther and farther away from the safety of Fenwick, she felt her cover slipping.

Change was not good. Not good for the plan.

What if his parents were in town and he was taking her to lunch, to meet them? It would be strange, since Parents' Day was in the spring, but it wasn't unheard of. And what if the Blakes recognized her somehow?

Or what if they were with the Pogues?

Laura's stomach dropped.

Stay calm, she ordered. As the car traveled farther from the campus, she closed her eyes. She could feel the soft cotton of Caleb's jacket, the rise and fall of his body as he breathed.

The car rolled to a stop a few minutes later.

"Hey, you asleep?"

Laura sat up. Sunlight streamed into the car through every window.

She looked around. They were at the mouth of a large field. A sign read FORT SAYBROOK MONUMENT PARK.

Relief washed over her.

Caleb paid the driver and grabbed her hand. "I know it's kind of lame, but when I interviewed at Fenwick my dad took me here afterward and we walked around. I always remembered it, but never really had a reason to come back." He swung her arm lightly, back and forth, as they walked down the gravel path and into the park. "But I thought you might be the one other person who'd appreciate it. Fort Saybrook was actually Connecticut's first military fortification—1635."

He's such a sweet guy. You should tell him the truth. He planned this whole surprise just for you and you're lying to him.

Laura ignored the black, ugly thoughts and instead sucked clean, sweet park air into her lungs. She looked up at the bright October sky. "It's not lame. It's beautiful here," she said. She squeezed Caleb's hand. "I love it."

He squeezed back. "I thought you would." He stopped walking and gave her arm a gentle tug, pulling her close. Then his hand was in her hair, combing the strands and teasing the back of her neck with the tips of his fingers.

"I wanted to make you happy," he said. His eyes were filled with the perfect mixture of softness and longing; the arm around her waist tightened.

Laura leaned in close to meet his lips. For once, she allowed the truth to rise.

"You do," she whispered.

32

No matter how poised and well-mannered
you are, the adventurous life of a Fabulous
Girl inevitably leads to a few
high-stakes dilemmas.
—*The Fabulous Girl's Guide to*
Grace Under Pressure
Kim Izzo, Ceri Marsh

There were days when Willa's cleaning schedule fell neatly into place. Days when she could coordinate the laundry with the vacuuming, waxing and polishing. The tasks fell away like dominos until she was the last man standing, triumphant amid a sparkling household, mop in one hand, Murphy Oil Soap in the other.

Today was not one of those days.

First of all, she'd accidentally set her alarm for 7 PM instead of 7 AM. Angie had left the house early, so Willa had overslept. She woke with a start at 8 AM and realized she was due at the Mortimers' house in fifteen minutes.

After a frenzied drive across town while brushing her teeth and hair, she'd made it there by eight-thirty. No real harm done. She worked her way through the house, then drove to the Watsons', sailing through a sea of green lights.

Things seemed to be looking up.

Willa finished the Watson mansion by three. She couldn't wait to get back to the apartment. After a lot of wrong turns— including dismantling and reassembling the car's engine—she and Angie had finally diagnosed Yellow Thunder. Its transmission was dying. They were, in fact, in the process of replacing it and *that* was going surprisingly well.

It turned out Angie had been right all along. Willa was a natural.

Jingling her car keys, Willa stepped out into the crisp fall air. Her fingers curled with anticipation. She could already feel the motor oil on her fingers, the grease under her nails. Nothing sounded better than the hum of an engine.

Willa frowned. Her hands dropped to her side.

There was a silver car blocking the station wagon. A 2007 Jaguar XJ8. She recognized the model immediately, having read about it in Angie's most recent issue of *AutoWeek*.

Willa looked back toward the house. She'd been through every room at least once. The place was deserted. Besides, didn't both Mr. and Mrs. Watson drive Mercedeses? She'd been pretty in tune with that sort of thing ever since NASCAR.

Well, one thing was certain. She wasn't going anywhere until the owner of the Jag returned. The car was parked on such a careless diagonal, they'd done an amazingly thorough job of boxing her in.

I could be here for hours, she thought. *Who parks like that?*

She took out her cell. The only new messages were, of course, IMs from Lubé:

```
lubespecial: ru there?
lubespecial: u there?
lubespecial: hey, did i really freak
u out that much by saying i want to mt
u? look i'm sorry. i take it back. i
don't want 2 mt u. if ur ever in CA
i'll alert border patrol, how's that?
lubespecial: 2 much? sorry. border
patrol doesn't usually return calls
anyway.
lubespecial: miss u, boardgirl.
```

Willa sighed. She had to deal, she knew she had to deal.

The problem was, she didn't know how. She'd never thought about actually meeting Lubé until he mentioned it. And his message had been flattering. No, it had been more than flattering. It had been thrilling. His IM—which she'd saved— had sent such a shock of excitement through her system, the response couldn't have been normal.

It was too much. It was too big. She couldn't handle it. *Not now.* Not when she wasn't even technically herself.

She shoved her phone back into her pocket. *Out of sight, out of mind.*

On the upside, she was standing in front of a Jaguar. She'd been dying to take a peek at some of the fancier cars, but all her clients kept their garages locked—and her parents always traveled with their cars. A little harmless investigating just might make the time fly.

What else was she supposed to do? She *was* stuck out here.

And the car was beautiful. It just sat there, sparkling and alone. A shiny silver dollar. Waiting for her.

The sun danced along the Jag's surface as Willa ran her hand over its smooth, polished curves. Her fingers wrapped around the pouncing cat, poised and frozen at the car's hood.

Pressing her face against the window, she memorized the car's rich interior: the power-adjustable driver's seat and leather-encased steering column, the miles of walnut paneling and the soft, deep leather seats.

I wonder if this engine is turbocharged or supercharged?

The article had said something about it, but she couldn't remember. And with high-performance engines it could go either way. She'd have to peek under the hood to find out.

But that was out of the question. If the owner saw her poking around underneath the hood of his or her car, well, it would be a bad thing. A very bad thing.

She could look *under* the car, though. There was no harm in that. Sure, it wasn't quite as satisfying as popping the hood, but it was definitely the less obvious exploration. At least this way she'd be concealed from anyone who pulled up. She'd hear them and would have ample time to roll away and then scramble to her feet.

She dropped down and scooted underneath the Jaguar. Using the flashlight from her key chain, she stared up at the car's insides. Her mouth fell open. She was used to the oxidized innards of Yellow Thunder, but this was beautiful. Not a drop of rust in sight.

I really hope the owner appreciates this car. And I really hope they drive better than they park, or else they're going to be a victim of road rage. Maybe—

"Um, excuse me? Is there a problem here?"

Willa slowly pushed her now smudged upper half out from under the Jaguar's body.

"Mrs. Watson, I'm really sorry." The words rolled off her tongue before her eyes adjusted to the light.

"Willa, is that *you?*"

She blinked and looked up. Her mother was standing next to Mrs. Watson, wearing her typical look of outrage. Outrage mingled with baffled disbelief.

Loxlike, flat on her back, Willa reviewed the million and one ways she could paint the blank canvas stretched before her. She *could*, for instance, pretend to be Laura and see if her mother fell for it. There was a chance it could work. She and her mother had never been all that close.

Or she could simply start to cry and play the sympathy card. Sometimes that helped. It might soften Mrs. Watson up, at the very least.

Willa sighed. In this type of situation, it was always best to go with your gut.

She peered up at the obviously perplexed Mrs. Watson and cleared her throat. Her voice was surprisingly calm and controlled.

"Your husband reads *Playboy,*" she announced. "*A lot* of *Playboy.*"

33

Dishgusted, dishgusted, dishgusted
—Lux Liquid

"Don't it always seem to go that you don't know what you've got till it's gone . . ."

Someone in Hubbard House loved Joni Mitchell. They also loved playing her songs at a deafeningly loud volume. As she approached the dorm after her last class, Laura could hear the pliant, girlish voice and free-spirited acoustic guitar from almost fifty feet away.

This particular song always made her tense. She couldn't help it. That chorus offended her.

It simply wasn't true. Not in her case, at least.

The trip to Fort Saybrook had been amazing. They'd hiked, eaten sandwiches outside a white clapboard house built in 1767 and strolled through what in the summer were lilac gardens but were now just patches of dirt and moss. It hadn't mattered, though. As long as she was with Caleb, a walking tour of Wal-Mart would seem beautiful.

They'd talked a lot that afternoon. Caleb had laughingly recounted his rocky elementary years: He'd almost failed nursery school for refusing to sit in the circle and then sent shock waves through kindergarten by telling his humorless teacher that he planned to be a giraffe when he grew up ("The whole cowboy thing just never appealed," he'd explained). The stories fascinated Laura. She drank them down; they became a part of her.

The day had brought them closer. More than ever, the two were always together. Or they were planning to be together.

She loved her life right now. At this very moment. She loved it all—Fenwick and Caleb and, okay, even Mr. Stade. The only reason the history teacher made her nervous in the first place was because he posed a potential threat to her, to the whole happy order.

No, as far as Laura was concerned, Joni Mitchell had no idea what she was talking about. Laura knew her life was special, that she was lucky to have it. She didn't need it to be ripped away from her to learn that.

Calm down, she reminded herself. *That song's not about you, remember? Isn't it about pesticides? Just forget it.*

Forcing herself to take a deep breath, she glanced up at the sky. Angry gray storm clouds floated overhead. She made a mental note to put an umbrella in her backpack. She was due to meet Caleb in front of the library and if it wasn't pouring by then it would start soon after.

Laura squeezed past a long black limousine that was parked just outside the dorm, blocking the steps.

She frowned. *Who parks like that?* she thought, rushing inside as the first crack of thunder licked the sky.

The Pogues parked like that.

They were all there, waiting for her: her mother, Mr. and Mrs. Pogue, Jenna Palmer—even the headmaster himself, Mr. Faber. And Willa, sitting between her parents, with red and teary eyes.

Willa met her gaze. "*Sorry,*" she mouthed.

Laura shook her head. "*It's okay,*" she mouthed back. And then, because it had been months and just the sight of her friend was enough to calm her shaking hands, she tacked on, "*I really missed you.*" Instinctively she went to hug her mom, but Mrs. Pogue cleared her throat and she stopped.

"I'm chairing a benefit with Ginger Watson," she began, glowering at Willa like this was somehow her fault as well. "We went to lunch the other day in Darien—she drove because I haven't quite gotten used to my new car. And when we returned to her house, imagine my surprise when I found my daughter *under* my car like some sort of low-level carjacker—"

"Um, Mom, that's not exactly how carjackers work—"

Willa trailed off as five pairs of angry eyes bore down on her. She dropped her gaze to the floor and studied the rug.

The Pogues were friends with the Watsons. Why hadn't it occurred to her—to either of them—that Willa's parents might be friends with at least one of the families on the cleaning roster? They'd thought they were being so clever. It was amazing they had made it this far. What a stupid, stupid, stupid plan.

Slowly, Laura looked up at her mother's pale, drained face.

She could feel the guilt everywhere now—her stomach, ears, toes.

Her mother turned her head away.

Mrs. Pogue opened up a brand-new lecture—and a fresh can of shock. She spoke of her own life at Willa's age, as a well-behaved, refined young woman and a perfect size two.

"Look, this is all my fault, okay?" Willa said suddenly. Her voice was shaky at first, then stabilized. "I just couldn't deal with another school, so just punish me, okay? I made Laura do it. I forced her—" She broke off, burying her face in her hands as she started to cry.

As the room fell silent, Laura drifted between two versions of herself. It would be so easy to let Willa take the fall. They would believe her. Willa would take all the blame and Laura's life would just silently, painlessly slide back to normal.

Only it wouldn't. She knew it wouldn't. If she were to become that person, she'd never be able to look in the mirror again. Or at Willa. Maybe, just maybe, her friend would give her a pass, forgive her for what she'd done. But Laura would hate herself forever.

No more lies. You just lose yourself.

"It's not true," she heard herself say. "I wanted to switch. Just for a while. I wanted a vacation from my life, too."

Reaching up to her face, Laura touched her cheeks. Hot, bright crimson. She knew it.

Laura Melon was back.

The headmaster cleared his throat. "Whatever your intentions, this is a very serious situation. Willa has missed almost an entire semester of school. And Laura, despite your strong performance at Fenwick, you're not a matriculated student." He gestured toward her mother. "From what we're told, you've

217

already received your high school diploma. After thoroughly discussing the matter, Ms. Palmer, the Pogues and I have all decided that the best course of action is for you to vacate the premises immediately," he continued, in a calm, firm monotone. "And quietly."

"We'll see that your belongings are forwarded to the proper address," Ms. Palmer added, in a tone of voice far too snooty for a grown woman wearing overalls.

Laura didn't bother to respond. She was sure Jenna Palmer had realized that everything in the room—from her clothing to her laptop—had all belonged to the Pogues. There would be no need for her to even leave a forwarding address.

Laura heard her mother thank the Pogues for being so understanding.

And then there was nothing left to say.

Laura turned to leave when she suddenly felt herself being swept into a bear hug.

"You've definitely been spending a lot of time with Angie," Laura whispered.

"You know it, Professor," Willa whispered back before rejoining her scowling parents.

34

Keep yourself quiet and composed under
all circumstances.
—*Manners, Etiquette and Deportment*
John Young, 1883

Here she was. Again. In the wood-paneled study, waiting for yet another rendition of the "what it means to be a Pogue" lecture.

What a shocker.

At least this time around the circumstances were different. It was strange, but Willa was actually feeling a bit optimistic. It was all relative, of course, but the other reprimands had been triggered by terrible exams and an overall poor school performance. This time, well—you can't have a GPA at a place you never attended in the first place.

So how bad could it be? Her parents didn't have all that much material to work with.

Willa pictured their cold, disapproving faces.

On second thought, her parents had always proven themselves to be surprisingly resourceful.

She shuddered.

The study door creaked open, causing her to sit up a little straighter.

It was Emory. He walked a few steps into the room, then seemed to notice Willa for the first time.

"Excuse me," he said. He stood rigid, his face sour. He looked like he'd just sat in something completely disgusting. He cleared his throat. "I had thought the room was empty. I didn't mean to disturb you."

Willa remembered her first morning at the Mortimers'. "Don't worry about it," she said. "Thank you for asking, though."

Emory froze, clearly unsure of where to place the sudden display of courtesy.

The study door snapped open and her parents marched in.

"Water, Emory," her mother snapped. "Still, not sparkling."

Emory turned. His eyes met Willa's. "Thank you," he said. And then he was gone.

"Appalling," her mother began. "Simply appalling." The drive home had been completely silent. Now the floodgates opened.

Her father cleared his throat. "You've lost an entire semester and, after this last stunt, have postponed graduation even further," he announced, staring down at her. "But what's even more troubling than your deplorable behavior is the fact that you have absolutely no goals or interests."

As her father's speech proceeded, Willa drew on her usual strategy: She held her body straight and alert while her mind reached for its thick, foggy slipcover. She had planned to tune in at the very end of the speech with some perfectly timed vow to do better. It was the way these wood-paneled discussions always unfolded.

But then she heard them. Those words: "you have absolutely no goals or interests."

A year ago, she would have let it go. Six months ago, even. Because back then it was true.

Not now. Now was a different story entirely.

"But you're wrong," she said, cutting her father off. "I do have interests. I—I'm sorry I interrupted you, but see, that's why I was under Mom's car in the first place. Weren't you even wondering about that?"

"I'm not sure I follow you." Her father was looking at her mother, his eyebrows raised.

Willa sighed. "Cars, Dad. Automobiles?"

Her parents stared at her with blank, hollow expressions.

Willa sighed. "Listen," she said, speaking slowly and enunciating every word. "I like cars. I like everything about them. I've been following NASCAR's *Chase for the Championship* and I've gotten kind of into it. I'm learning all about cars, too—race cars and regular ones. I replaced a transmission the other day—well, this other girl and I did it together." She took a deep breath, her eyes shining with excitement. "I really think—I mean, I have a lot to learn—but I think I could work the racing circuit one day. You know, on a pit crew. The thing is, well, I think I'm really good at this."

Willa paused and stared up at her parents. To say they looked shocked was an understatement.

Slowly, Willa felt her spirit deflate. *I should've known better. Why even try?*

"The thing is," her mother started, "I think you've forgotten once again who you are. As a Pogue you have a responsibility . . ."

But Willa was no longer listening. Instead, her thoughts had turned to Angie. Angie had said they were family and, in a weird way, they had been. Willa's former roommate had supported and encouraged her in a way that her own parents never had. Maybe it simply wasn't their way, but at the moment, that didn't seem like much of an excuse.

And just like that, something inside her snapped. An engine roared. Tires squealed. Spark plugs fired.

I've done my time, she decided.

"You know what?" Willa said, standing. "I *hate* being a Pogue. Why do you think I even switched places with Laura in the first place? I was happier scrubbing bathrooms and floors— as someone else—than I ever was being a Pogue." She turned to her mother. "Whatever happened with the ballet? Did you stop dancing because you married a *Pogue?*"

Her mother gaped at her. "I'm sure I don't . . . ," she started, then seemed to lose her place midthought.

"Willa, sit down!" her father yelled. "Your behavior is atrocious."

Willa ignored him. Her mother's eyes had taken on a deep, far-off cast. "Because if that's why you stopped," Willa pressed, "I mean, if you really loved it—that's kind of pathetic, right? 'Cause I think, well, maybe all of our dead relatives would forgive you." Fat, salty tears rolled down her cheeks and into her mouth. "And even if they didn't, who really cares anyway? They're dead."

This time around she didn't wait for a reaction. Voices floated around her but it was too late for that now. Willa stood and pushed through the door without looking back, leaving her parents in the wood-paneled study alone with her words.

35

It's so hard to say good-bye.
—Febreze

When the headmaster had told Laura to vacate the premises immediately, he hadn't been joking.

As soon as she and her mother left her dorm room, two campus security guards met them in the hall and escorted them to the station wagon.

Not that the act was particularly menacing. The guards' combined age probably teetered somewhere around one hundred and sixty. But Laura got the point. Anyway, it didn't matter. She was in no mood to hang around. And she doubted her mother would be interested in a campus tour.

It had stopped raining and as she walked, Laura kept her eyes glued to the slick, wet pavement. If she couldn't be a part of Fenwick anymore, maybe she could forget it had ever existed in the first place.

"Willa!"

The voice that echoed across the quad caused Laura to freeze midstep.

"Willa!"

Her heart twisted in her chest. That voice didn't belong to her anymore. Even so, she couldn't seem to move.

"Miss, we really should be moving along," said the older of the two security guards. His tone was gentle.

Laura looked up. Caleb was less than fifty feet away from her. He was looking at her, at the security guards and at her mother. She could see his mind trying to wrap around the situation.

"Willa?"

And then Caleb froze. He wasn't looking at her anymore. He was looking past her and his face had paled.

Laura turned her head slightly, even though she already knew what—or who—was there.

Willa Pogue and her parents. The real deal.

Laura ran to the car.

"Mom," she said, her voice catching in her throat, "I'm so sorry. I'm sorry you had to cut your trip short. I'm sorry about everything. I honestly never meant to hurt anyone. Neither of us did."

"I know," her mother said softly, her eyes moist. "But I just . . . I feel like I don't know you, Laura. I feel like the Laura I raised wouldn't do something like this." She shook her head as her hands gripped the steering wheel. "Sure, I know maybe the work we do isn't glamorous, but I thought you were proud of our life. I know I was always so proud of *you*."

Laura stared at her feet. "I guess I just wanted to see what someone else's life was like for a while. Sort of escape. It didn't seem all that complicated at the time."

"Dreams are important. Why do you think I play the Lotto and spend so much time entering sweepstakes?" Laura's mother turned to her, her face serious. "But there's a big difference between playing the lottery and stealing the award money. Don't you see that? And I know you didn't mean to—I know you and Willa made a deal—it certainly wasn't malicious or anything. But whether you intended to or not, you did steal."

Months ago, Laura had called Willa a spoiled brat. But she was spoiled too. Selfish and spoiled. She'd let everyone down. Her mother. Caleb. Mr. Stade. None of them had deserved this.

When they got home, Laura raised herself out of the car and followed her mother inside. She trudged through the apartment as if in a trance and headed straight to her room. She wanted— no she needed—her bed. Now. She was too depressed to do anything else. Her head was throbbing.

"Hey, Professor! Come on in!" Angie boomed as she swept her into a hug. "I did a little cleaning 'cause your mom said she'd probably bring you back with her." Angie dropped her onto the ground with one arm and waved her into the room with the other. "I'd been sleeping in her room for months, but now that she's back, I guess you and me, we're officially roommates, huh?"

Laura looked around, surprised to find that Angie had been incredibly respectful of her space. Her half of the room was exactly as she'd left it, while only Angie's side was wallpapered with pictures of Yellow Thunder and various types of above- and belowground swimming pools.

Laura sank down onto the bed and stared up at the ceiling. "I guess you heard about all the trouble Willa and I got into," she said. She wondered if Angie was planning on rescinding her nickname. After today, it seemed sort of unlikely that anyone would think she was smart.

Angie nodded. "I heard," she said, lying back on her own bed. "You know, I got to tell you, I figured out that girl wasn't you awhile back."

"Wait. What?" Laura jerked up and swung her legs around. "Did Willa tell you?"

Angie laughed. "Take it easy, Professor. Nothing like that."

"Then what? How did you know?"

"You guys are real look-alikes, that's for sure." Angie gazed fondly at a picture of Yellow Thunder. "Only, that girl was like a class A mechanic. You should have seen her." She smiled at the memory. "And the only time I showed you Yellow Thunder, no offense, well—you were all thumbs."

Laura closed her mouth, which she hadn't realized was hanging open. "I don't get it," she said, shaking her head. Why wasn't Angie strangling her? Why wasn't she looking at her like she was a criminal? "You were living with a stranger for months. Weren't you mad? Didn't you want to say something?"

Angie shrugged. "Nope. It's not really my style to nose around," she said. "Like I said before, I like her. I like you, too. Either way, I had a cool roommate." She looked at Laura. "And you know, when your mom told me the whole story I got it right away. I could see why you switched, you know? I can't blame you guys for that."

"Why not?" Laura said. Of all the exchanges she'd had today, this was by far the most baffling.

Angie shrugged like the answer was written on Laura's headboard. "Everyone wishes they were someone else once in a while."

Laura stared at her. Angie, she realized, was much more of a "professor" than she was. "Angie," she said, "would you have done what Willa and I did?"

Angie tossed her head back and laughed. "Probably not. But you know, I get to live my dream all the time—or at least whenever Yellow Thunder's up and running." She pointed to the picture of the car and sighed. "Ol' Yellow really makes me feel like I'm racing for NASCAR."

Laura leaned back against her pillows. Angie's Trans Am, her mother's lottery tickets. Everyone around her had found their own little secret, their own escape. What was wrong with her?

Angie glanced down at her watch. "I gotta go," she said. "I got a green-water situation all the way out in Kent." She stood and stretched, cracking her knuckles high overhead. It sounded like someone was cooking up microwave popcorn in front of a bullhorn. "Listen," she said, "you and Willa are gonna be okay."

"Thanks, Angie."

Angie paused at the door. "Maybe, you know, we could all hang out sometime."

"I'd really like that," Laura said. And as the words spilled out of her mouth, she was surprised by how much she meant them.

36

Curled up on her window seat, Willa stared out at the leaf-covered lawn and considered the old adage: Before you can understand a person, you've got to walk a mile in his shoes. She understood that the advice implied empathy. It was supposed to show you how other people lived—how difficult the other guy had it. But the saying was supposed to make you appreciate your own life, too. After walking that mile you were expected to request—no, beg for—your shoes back.

And that was where she and the cliché parted company.

As far as Willa was concerned, it simply didn't apply to her situation. She'd not only walked a mile in someone else's shoes, she'd vacuumed, mopped and scrubbed in them. And after she'd done all those things, she hadn't missed her old shoes at all. She hadn't even been curious as to their whereabouts.

Not that any of it mattered anymore. Her parents were going to stuff her back into her hideous, uncomfortable, ill-fitting shoes and ship her off to Fenwick. Or maybe a military academy. They'd probably fly her everywhere from now on, too—since cars were bound to be considered a bad influence.

Sunlight tumbled in through the window and stretched across Willa's legs in thick, fat stripes. As she hugged her knees to her chest, Willa's eyes traced the lines where they fell across the floor. Her brain skipped forward and settled on Laura.

Why hadn't Laura let her take the blame? Everything was her fault. The whole plan had been her idea. She groaned into her knees as the image of Mrs. Melon's red, injured face flashed through her mind. It would haunt her forever.

Her stomach rumbled, but there was no way she was going down to the kitchen for a snack. She'd rather starve. She deserved it. She deserved worse.

She was so depressed and weary that she didn't hear the knock on her door.

So she was genuinely surprised—shocked, even—when her mother slipped quietly into the room. It had been years since either of her parents had been inside. So long, in fact, that Willa wondered if her mom had gotten lost on the way to her wing of the house.

Her mother sat at the foot of her bed and tilted her head slowly to one side, as if testing the mobility of her neck.

"So," she said. Her voice was so quiet that Willa had to lean forward slightly to hear. "You found my ballet memorabilia. I'm still in shock."

"It was kind of an accident." Willa looked at her, not sure whether to go on. Her mother didn't *look* mad. She didn't look happy, but she definitely didn't look mad. "It was when I was, uh, pretending to be Laura. I was in the cellar."

"I did love it, you know." A hint of light crept into her mother's eyes. "My parents sent me to weekly lessons when I was small. It was what one did." She glanced at Willa. "We sent you, do you remember?"

Willa avoided her mother's gaze. Her ballet teacher, Miss Audrey, had suggested Willa "take some time off" after she'd spent her entire first recital picking her nose—center stage—while the rest of her class had danced around her.

"It didn't really take," Willa said.

Her mother didn't seem to hear. "From the minute my hand slid over the barre, I was in love." Her voice sounded far away. "By the time I was ten I was studying four times a week after school."

"Wow, that's pretty . . . intense." With every second, her mother was looking more and more like the slim young girl from those black-and-white pictures.

"It was. And I think my parents admired my discipline." She looked at her lap. "They attended my performances and tried to be supportive. But when I informed them that I wanted to pursue dance professionally . . ." She trailed off.

Willa frowned. "I can't imagine Grandmother or Grandfather Welles really being fans of the idea."

Her mother lifted her head. "No," she said, her voice flat. "They weren't. It wasn't proper. I was scheduled for a debutante ball, slated for college, marriage to the right man." She sighed.

"Ballet was to have been a passing fancy. This definitely threw them for a loop." She smiled and Willa thought she saw—she couldn't be sure—a hint of mischief flash across her face.

Is she saying she didn't want to marry Dad? Willa wondered. *Is she saying her whole life has been a big disappointment?*

But she kept those questions to herself.

"So what did you do?"

Her mother straightened. "We went back and forth for months, until I finally decided that I'd had enough of society living. I withdrew some money from my trust and moved to New York. I planned to join the American Ballet Theatre." She looked, Willa thought, both bemused and sad. "Just like that."

Willa stared at her. "Whoa," she breathed. She tried to imagine her mother as a young woman, living alone in Manhattan, but her mind refused to form the image.

Her mother looked down at her lap. "It was not a successful trip," she said. "I got to the audition, and the steps—I'd never seen anything like it before. I couldn't follow. I lasted all of three minutes."

"Mom, I'm so sor—"

But her mother didn't hear her. She'd stepped back inside the moment, like no time had passed at all. "That's when I knew that starring in my ballet school's production of *Coppélia* was the best I could ever hope for." Her voice shook slightly and Willa felt her heart thicken. "I could study fourteen hours a day, but I was never going to be a professional dancer."

Willa swallowed. "I'm sorry, Mom."

Her mother ran a hand through her ink-black hair, as if wiping away the unpleasant memories. When she spoke, her voice was clipped and measured. "It was a lesson," she said. "Frankly, I consider myself lucky to have only wasted an afternoon, rather than an entire year. Maybe two." She cleared her throat. "As it happened, I gathered my things and hopped on the first train back to Newport. I applied to college and met your father the following spring."

Willa straightened, unsure of how to react. So what was her mother saying? That she should run back to Fenwick and look for a husband? That she should listen to her mother because her parents had been right thirty years ago?

Her mother leaned forward. Her hair looked almost blue in the sunlight. She seemed to soften slightly. "Willa, I love your father. And I was a good debutante. I know that sort of thing is lost on young people nowadays, but, well, when I was younger it meant something. In the end I don't regret the choices I've made because, unlike dance, I really do excel at fund-raising and the occasional game of mixed doubles."

Willa eyed her mother. Was that a joke? It was, wasn't it? Her mother's eyes held that same mischievous glint.

Unbelievable.

"What you said downstairs—about fixing your friend's car— was that true?"

"I was the one who diagnosed the problem," Willa explained. "Angie—she's the girl who owns the car—knew it was making a weird noise but she couldn't figure out what was going on. I told her." Her voice rose proudly as she spoke. "Of course, that was only after I played jigsaw puzzle with her engine. I kind of owed her one."

"You know," her mother said slowly, "if I had been a talented dancer it might have been a different story. The whole trajectory of my life—who knows?" She seemed to shake herself. "And while your chosen pursuit is certainly out of the ordinary—at least for this family—a talent is a talent. . . ."

Willa's jaw dropped open as her mind spiraled off into a million different places at once.

Pay attention. This is important.

"I had always hoped you'd find your way academically. Or perhaps on the athletic field," her mother continued. "But after this past semester we see now that that might never happen. It's still very important to your father and me that you finish school, though," she said firmly. "Not because you're a Pogue but because you're our daughter. Do you understand?"

Willa nodded.

"Good. Here's our offer," her mother said. Her tone left no room for negotiation. "You can stay home and attend the local high school starting next semester. Your father and I will stay here with you, full-time." She studied Willa closely for any signs of rebellion. "In return, you are to attend—and pass—all your courses."

"Public school?" The words flew out of Willa's mouth before she could stop them.

"I hear it's quite good." Her mother stood and smoothed out her skirt. "Besides, I'm sure they'll have some sort of 'shop' elective you can take. If you're going to pursue this as an interest, you might as well go about it properly. At the very least, I'd like to see you fixing fine automobiles." She sniffed. "It just seems less coarse, somehow."

Willa grinned.

Her mother cast a stern look in her direction.

"But your GPA has to improve, Willa. If it doesn't, the deal is off."

"Right."

In a forgotten corner of her heart, Willa felt a quiver. It was so unfamiliar—strange, in fact—this fresh swell of emotion. Odd but pleasant.

"Thank you," she said. Her voice was hoarse. "Thanks, Mom."

Her mother gave her a funny half nod, half smile. Willa watched her mother's thin, graceful back ease its way across the floor. And then—Willa was never sure but she could've sworn—as her mother stepped out the door, her toes were pointed.

Willa settled back into the window seat. She hesitated only a second before scooping up the shiny silver phone at her feet.

```
boardgirl: i'm so, so sorry. messed
everything up. my life has been
really screwed up, u have no idea.
lubespecial: try me.
```

37

Choose your Cheer.
—Cheer Detergent

"Professor? Where are you?"

Laura tried to shake off her daze and turned toward Angie. "I'm sorry. What were you saying?"

"Nothing important." Angie rose from behind Yellow Thunder's raised hood, her brow furrowed. "You okay? You seem a little out of it."

Laura shook her head. "No, it's okay. I'm just tired. It's hard starting work again and everything."

Willa shoved herself out from underneath the car's body. Her face was covered with thick black grease. "I think I found the leak," she said. "Or at least one of them." She paused. "Wait, what'd I miss?"

Angie motioned toward Laura with an oily rag. "Professor's sad."

"Not true. I'm really not."

"You should call that guy, Laura," Willa said. She wiped her face and hands on a bandana. "I know that's what's bothering you."

"Or how about a present?" Angie suggested. "I love those cards—you know, the ones that play music. Or chocolate. Everyone loves chocolate."

Laura sighed. Now that Willa's life had taken an upward swing, she was hanging out at the apartment a lot. She and Angie were using the time to work on Yellow Thunder—and offer Laura advice. It was all well-intended, of course. And Laura was appreciative that Willa had forgiven her for amending the "plan" to include a boyfriend—without even so much as a consultation. But things with Caleb were past the point of a Whitman's Sampler and singing greeting cards.

Almost two weeks had passed since the Fenwick disaster. She'd considered contacting Caleb—she'd even picked up the phone a few times. But then she'd remembered how they left things—his pale, horrified expression and her panicked retreat—and she couldn't follow through. Besides, what was she supposed to say? *I'm sorry I repeatedly lied to you for four months. I'm sorry I'm just a housecleaner.*

Anyway, she barely had time to call. She'd thrown herself back into her old life—her *real* life—without looking back.

She'd started by finishing her UConn application. As she'd stood in line at the post office, she'd glanced down at the envelopes, not recognizing her own handwriting. It was angrier than usual—fierce, deep slashes that practically sliced the page.

Why am I so bitter? she wondered. She ran her fingers over the grooves in disbelief. *UConn is a good school. It's where I'd planned to go all along, before the switch.*

Before.

That was it, wasn't it? Deep down, there'd been a part of her that really had believed—or hoped—that there would be no "after." She'd always harbored some insane fantasy that the switch would be permanent. There was nothing at all wrong with UConn. But by mailing off her application, Laura felt like she'd somehow returned to a life—and a self—she'd already waved good-bye to.

By the time Laura had approached the window, she'd smudged the return address. The elderly postal worker offered her a tissue. Laura hadn't realized she was crying.

She was also cleaning again. Every house minus two: the Pogues' (for obvious reasons, they'd made arrangements to use another service) and the Youngs'. For less obvious reasons, Willa refused to relinquish that job. It wasn't about the money. She promised to give that to Laura's mom. She simply insisted that the place "sort of felt like home."

Still, even without those houses it was a pretty packed schedule. It was, in fact, her old schedule. It was the way she used to live.

And that was the problem. Her old life didn't fit anymore. She'd unhitched herself from it months ago, slipped it off like an old coat. And in the interim, pieces of the last few months—the conversations, smells and experiences—had all joined hands inside her. And so, despite the sameness, Laura herself was changed. She wanted to wear her coat again—she needed to, in fact. But she couldn't. She couldn't even find the closet.

And she couldn't, for whatever stupid reason, cheer *up*.

Floating back to earth, Laura looked over at Willa and Angie. They were staring at her expectantly and she realized they were still waiting for her to respond to their advice.

"I'll think about it," she said. "Thanks, guys. I know you're trying to help." It was her trademark response, but her friends never pushed. "I'm gonna go inside and read a little. I'll see you later?"

Willa waved before she disappeared back under the car. "Sure, I'll stop in before I leave. Listen, give yourself a break, okay?"

Laura went inside. The phone was ringing as she unlocked the door. "Mom?" she shouted. She wasn't in the mood to deal. "Mom?"

Laura stood in the kitchen as the phone's shrill bleat cracked the air. Why wasn't the machine picking up?

She sighed and leaned over, grabbing the receiver.

"Hello?"

"Hello, Laura?"

It was Mr. Stade. Laura swallowed the last remaining moisture in her mouth as recognition kicked the air out of her lungs.

"Yes."

Why was Mr. Stade calling her? Laura wondered. Did he want a personal apology? Was he furious at her for wasting all his time? Should she simply hang up and refuse to speak with him?

No. No, that was lame. She had to deal. This was her fault. She should've told him the truth months ago. At the very least, she should talk to him. She owed him that much.

"I hope you don't mind that I'm calling you."

"No. No, not at all," she said. She took the first deep breath she'd taken since picking up the phone. "Listen, I don't really know what to say. I know what I did was—well, horrible. But it really started because of Fenwick. I kind of fell in love with the place." She sighed. "I know it doesn't change anything, but I just wanted you to know that. You really were the best teacher I've ever had." She paused. "Even if you weren't officially my teacher."

There was a silence on the other end of the line.

"Thank you, Laura," he said. "And thank you for your apology. I have to say, I was a little upset to hear about what you'd done. On the other hand, I wasn't as shocked as you might think."

Laura's forehead wrinkled. "Wait, what do you mean?"

"Well, let's just say that I've been teaching for almost twenty years and I'd never seen a student do such a rapid turnaround, performance-wise, in my entire career." Mr. Stade chuckled. "Not even when college counselors were breathing down her neck."

"I don't understand. Why didn't you tell the headmaster? Or the Pogues?"

"What would I have said? And to be honest, you were a joy to have in class," he explained. "Plus, I don't think I've ever seen anyone go to such extreme lengths to receive a good education. You're an incredibly dedicated student."

"Thanks," Laura said. "I'm sorry," she added lamely.

"Thank you, Laura, but I really wasn't calling for an apology." He cleared his throat. "I wanted you to know that there's no reason why I can't continue to advise—or pester—you about your college choices simply because you're no longer *my* student. And I'd still like to call my friend at Kenyon, with your permission, of course."

It was such a nice gesture, Laura thought. Too bad she had to turn him down.

"The thing is," she explained, "I'd love to go to Kenyon, or any of the other colleges you suggested. That was never the problem." She swallowed. "See, I don't have any money. College is a stretch if I want to attend full-time, without racking up so much debt my mom—" She broke off as her throat closed. She was crying now. "Thanks so much," she said, her stomach hollow. "But that's just not my life. I'm a housecleaner, not a prep school kid."

"Laura," he said, "sometimes a person's real life is the life they don't lead. Have you ever thought about that?"

"No." Fresh tears spilled onto the receiver. "I—I'm not even sure I know what that means."

"Yes, you do. It's a great quote." He laughed. "Of course, it's not *my* great quote—Oscar Wilde said it. But I'm sure he wouldn't mind my using it in this situation. The point is, I don't know Laura the housecleaner, but I do know Laura the Fenwick student. And maybe you weren't officially matriculated, but don't you think your campus life was real? It certainly seemed real to me."

"I guess so," Laura said, sniffling. But the more she thought about it, the more she knew he was right. Her life on campus had been real.

"I think that the person you were in my classroom—and that life you were leading—was one you'd led for years, Laura. In one way or another."

Laura straightened.

"My advice is simple," he continued. "If something is important to you—really important—don't let it go so easily. Some things are worth a little fight." He paused. "No matter how scared you are."

Laura thanked Mr. Stade. She also agreed to speak with him in the next few days about colleges—and financial aid.

But as they hung up, his words rang in her ears—over and over again: *Some things are worth a little fight. No matter how scared you are.*

That was when she started to run toward the parking lot.

"I have to go," she shouted at Angie's back and Willa's legs.

"I'm leaving for Fenwick," she called as the girls hoisted themselves out of Yellow Thunder and stared at her in confusion. "Right now."

38

Put the freshness back.
—Shake n' Vac

Maybe this wasn't such a great idea after all, she thought as she parked outside Caleb's dorm room.

Laura's anxiety existed on three levels. First of all, her plan wasn't really much of a plan. She had no idea what she was going to say once she saw Caleb. She had to apologize, but how? She'd tried to rehearse during the drive, but her mind was a sieve.

Second, she wasn't supposed to be back on campus. It was part of the arrangement—when she'd left last time, she'd left for good. If campus security caught her, she'd be in serious trouble.

The last leg of her distress had to do with the fact that the station wagon had been unavailable for the trip. Laura had wanted to leave immediately and her mother had been out mailing her Chillin' for a Million sweepstakes ballot. Angie needed the Dr. Pool van in case any emergency calls came in and so, much to Laura's horror, she'd been forced to drive Yellow Thunder to Fenwick. Willa and Angie had both lent her their AAA cards—just in case.

Laura climbed out of the car and glanced up at Caleb's

window. His light was on. He was probably in his room, packing for Thanksgiving break. Her heart pounding, she crossed the slick, grassy island that stretched between the pavement and the back of the dorm. Moonlight danced over her as she slipped around the side of the building and in through an open fire door.

Campus security is so pathetic, she thought.

She peeled down the hall and knocked once on Caleb's door before she had time to process what she'd done.

Still clenched, her hand froze. From deep inside, sharp warning bells sounded. *Save yourself the pain.*

It was true. Caleb hadn't tried to get in touch once since she'd left school. True, he didn't have her number, but he did have Willa's. She'd assumed he was too angry to call. Or hurt. But it suddenly occurred to her that maybe she'd been flattering herself. Maybe he'd simply moved on.

And then, just like that, Caleb's door swung open.

Laura smiled. She couldn't help herself.

Only this time, Caleb didn't return the favor. He moved aside, allowing Laura to enter.

Well, that's something, she thought. *He could've kicked me out.*

There was an open suitcase on his bed. Caleb shoved it aside and sat down.

"Well, this is a big surprise," he said. His voice was cold. "Or wait, which one are you? I think that this time around, I should know from the start. I did help one of you with your schedule."

Laura ignored his tone. She took a deep breath and forced herself to start—slowly and calmly—from the very beginning. She spread out her life—her real life—as neatly as a tablecloth. She explained her childhood and how, over the years, her bitterness and resentment had grown until she couldn't appreciate any of the things that she had. And her look-alike, Willa Pogue, had been in the exact same frame of mind when they'd met. The plan had grown from there.

Through it all Caleb sat in silence, his face closed.

"You weren't a part of it," Laura said. Her cheeks burned, not the usual apple-red sign of embarrassment, but a deep, nettling pain that cut down through her chest. "I wasn't supposed to meet someone like you. I wasn't supposed to meet anyone. I—I just wanted to be like the people who I worked for—just for a while, you know?"

She was so sick of crying, but she couldn't seem to stop. Caleb looked up at her and, for the first time, Laura noticed the deep purple smudges underneath his eyes. He hadn't been sleeping.

"The thing is," he said, slowly, "the person I fell in love with doesn't even exist."

Laura straightened. "It's not true," she said. "When I was with you, that was *me*." She looked at him, her eyes wide with apology. "I wanted to tell you. I almost did so many times. I was just worried that when you found out who I was—you know, my family—you'd think—"

Caleb shook his head. "I don't get it," he cut in. "I mean, I thought you failed out of school. I thought you were like a bribe away from prep school delinquent. If that didn't bother me, then why would you think the other stuff would? How big of a snob do you think I am?"

"No! It's just—I really underestimated you." Laura shook her head. "I'm sorry. I think I was scared. It's just that—well, it's easy for you. You grew up in the circle. I grew up outside the circle . . . well, actually I cleaned the circle, which is kind of worse because you—"

Caleb groaned. "Laura, I don't know what circle you're talking about," he said. "But you're being ridiculous. I don't want to be with your *name*. I never did." He looked at her. "You really didn't even give me a chance, that's what kills me."

"I'm sorry," she said, sniffling. "I know. You have every right to hate me. I messed up."

"I know. And to be honest, I never liked the name Pogue all that much. It's stupid."

He was coming toward her now, closing the distance. His hand lifted her chin as his lips fell softly over hers. Laura's heart fluttered.

She pulled away. "Are you sure?"

Caleb laughed. "No. Not at all." He kissed her again, long and deep. Laura felt the worry ebb as she moved her body against his.

"I'm sure, okay?" he said, his mouth against her ear as his hand reached up and toyed with her ponytail.

"So," she said, "this is what it's like to feel rich."

Caleb shrugged. "I guess so. I didn't know, until I met you." He squinted as he looked through the window just over her head. "Hey, is that your Trans Am out in the parking lot?"

39

Once she no longer has to act demure and ladylike, the opportunities for a postdeb's social life (and love life) are endless.
—*The Debutante's Guide to Life*

Six Months Later

lubespecial: so ur really coming?
boardgirl: totally. Spring break. Flight 2176, arrives SF 5:25 PM.
lubespecial: i can't believe it.
boardgirl: me neither. and can't believe we convinced my mom that i won't be abducted by a gang of west coast hippies. plse thank ur mom 4 talking 2 her, ok? she actually apologized after she hung up. a major first.
lubespecial: no prob. they bonded. had no idea ur mom is golf nut 2. they swapped pointers. thrilling.

boardgirl: no more golf talk, ok?

lubespecial: good rule. c u soon willa pogue

boardgirl: u 2, lucas bennet

•

To Do List—W. Pogue

* HOMEWORK: just do it. Ask Laura and Caleb for help with precalculus – DO NOT let that grade slip below a C!
* CAR STUFF: change oil, Dad's car
* Mom and Dad – one more appeal for my own Mustang convertible (no, it's not coarse . . . and I'll even raise my GPA up to a B . . . okay, B minus)
* Question Angie re: Yellow Thunder – WHY the grinding? We just changed the clutch. . . . Is she shifting too hard???

SPRING BREAK SHOPPING: vintage!

* Defend clothing purchases to Mom, explain that they don't need to be fumigated by Terminix Pest Control.
* YOUNGS: more Swiffer Wet refills. Remind them about my vacation . . .
* Confirm seat assignment/San Francisco flight. (Get Lube's mom's cell in event of extreme emergency? She and Mom seem to be BFF.)
* Hair apptmt – dye? No dye? Hmmmm . . .
* Present for Lube's family? Mom suggested Godiva but that's so . . . old me.

40

Lock in the freshness.
—Ziploc Storage Bags

Wesleyan University
Middletown, CT
Foster H. Hillman House

Dear Laura,

It is with great pleasure that we welcome
you to the class of 2012! After careful review
of your application, we are pleased to offer
you the Foster H. Hillman Scholarship. This
academic scholarship is offered each year to
one incoming freshman whose scholastic
record and teacher recommendations im-
press the Wesleyan admissions committee.
Please note that this scholarship extends
throughout the course of your four-year
tenure at Wesleyan.

Once more, we wish to congratulate you on

this very prestigious award. We welcome you to the Wesleyan community!

Best,

William H. Hadley
Executive Director
Foster H. Hillman Scholarship

Caleb — So it looks like I'll be able to go after all! How far did you say Wesleyan was from Brown? ☺